THE RELUCTANT ANGEL

G000269545

'Falling in love with Drew is like the measles—*all* the nurses catch a bout and all of them recover.' But for young Staff Nurse Sandie Masters, love for enigmatic surgeon Drew Maxwell has only one cure—and though Drew is tempted, he seems unwilling to proceed with the treatment!

THE RELUCTANT ANGEL

BY

SARAH FRANKLIN

MILLS & BOON LIMITED
15–16 BROOK'S MEWS
LONDON W1A 1DR

First published in Great Britain 1984
by Mills & Boon Limited

© Sarah Franklin 1984

Australian copyright 1984
Philippine copyright 1984

ISBN 0 263 74887 1

Set in 11 on 12 pt Linotron Times
03/1284–53,000

Photoset by Rowland Phototypesetting Ltd
Bury St Edmunds, Suffolk
Made and printed in Great Britain by
Richard Clay (The Chaucer Press) Ltd
Bungay, Suffolk

CHAPTER ONE

'I HOPE you won't mind a spell on Intensive Care.'

Sandie Masters glanced at the Senior Nursing Officer walking beside her along the corridor. It was her first day at Hartmoor General Hospital and her head was still spinning from all that she had been shown in the last half-hour. Hartmoor was a much larger hospital than the small teaching establishment in the Midlands where she had done her training. Set in several acres of neatly kept grounds, its ten storeys rose, white and gleaming, to tower over the little market town in the Cotswolds where Sandie and her stepmother had moved a month ago after Sandie's father's death.

She shook her head. 'I'd quite welcome it. After I qualified six months ago my first job as staff nurse was on Intensive Care. I liked it so much I was seriously thinking about taking a special course in it before we moved.'

Mary Crawford smiled sympathetically. 'It was bad luck for you, losing your father and having to move just after you qualified. You must find it very different here to the Midlands. Still, we're certainly glad to have you and I'm sure you'll find the work interesting.'

They went up in the lift to the sixth floor, then along another short corridor to the Intensive Care ward where Sandie was introduced to Sister

Milton, whose quick eyes took in the trim figure and neatly coiled hair with obvious approval.

'Welcome to Hartmoor General. I'm delighted to have you,' she smiled. 'I've been struggling without a staff nurse for the past week, since Nurse Collins went sick.'

Mary Crawford laughed. 'Don't let that put you off! It wasn't overwork, just a bad attack of tonsillitis.' She glanced across the ward to a cubicle where a third year nurse was busy stripping a bed. 'That's Nurse Sammes. She lives at the nurses' home too. Perhaps when you go for your lunch-break Sister will let her go with you and show you the places I haven't had time to cover.'

The Intensive Care ward at Hartmoor was very much more modern than the one Sandie had been used to. Each bed was in a separate glass-walled cubicle, all within view of the central desk. As Sister Milton pointed out, the glass partitions helped to cut down the risk of cross infection.

'Of course, as you know, we don't have patients here for very long,' she reminded Sandie. 'Usually only three to four days, either pre- or post-op. But we do have a variety of different cases and one never knows what will come in from one hour to the next. At present we have only four, and two of those are due to be moved out at any time.'

She took Sandie round to familiarise her with the four, reacquainting her as they went with the equipment of intensive care—monitors, ventilators and the various other forms of life support. As they completed the round she glanced at her watch.

'Doctors' rounds at any minute. Come with

me while I take the routine blood samples and observations. After that it'll be all yours.'

The checks were meticulously carried out and the results noted on each patient's chart. The two who were almost ready to be moved to general wards were conscious, though still sedated; one, an accident victim with a head injury, the other, recovering from facial surgery. They were just finishing when the young blonde nurse touched Sister's arm.

'May I go for my break now, Sister?'

Sister Milton looked at her watch and gasped. 'Good heavens, child! You should have gone half an hour ago. Why didn't you remind me? It'll be doctors' rounds at any minute.' She pursed her lips. 'Oh well, as I have a new staff nurse I suppose it's all right. If you don't go now you won't get your break at all. Off you go then.'

But a few moments later, as she was showing Sandie where to find the key to the drugs cupboard, she looked up from her desk and gave a muffled exclamation as she saw two white-coated figures coming in through the ward doors.

'Oh no! It's Mr Maxwell *and* Mr Crabtree! They would have to arrive together just when I've sent Nurse Sammes off for her break. Isn't it always the way?' She looked at Sandie. 'I hate to push you in at the deep end, but I'm afraid I shall have to ask you to go with Mr Maxwell. I have some urgent notes for Mr Crabtree. Mr Maxwell is the consultant neurosurgeon and I'm afraid he has rather a short fuse at times, but he's really very nice, so you mustn't mind if he's a bit short with you.'

Pink-faced and breathless, she hurried out of the

office to greet the two consultants. Following close behind her, Sandie looked at them. One was a small, wiry man of about fifty, with thin, greying hair and a benign smile; the other was younger—in his late thirties, tall and broad, with uncompromising dark grey eyes. His dark hair had a distinctive silver streak winging back above his right temple. Sister rushed forward, smiling placatingly at him.

'Oh, Mr Maxwell, I hope you don't mind, but I have some important notes for Mr Crabtree. Staff Nurse Masters will see that you have everything you want.' She stepped aside, revealing Sandie, whom the consultant appraised briefly.

'Right—thank you, Sister.' He turned and walked across to where Peter Marshall, the young accident victim lay. Sandie had just had time to note from the boy's chart that he had suffered contusions of the brain following a skull fracture, but was now on the mend and out of danger.

As Drew Maxwell looked down at his patient his rather forbidding features softened into a smile and Sandie was quite startled at the transformation.

'Good morning, Peter. How are you feeling today? Well, you'll be happy to know that I've seen your latest X-rays and they show a great improvement. Would it cheer you up to know that we're moving you down to Men's Surgical this afternoon?'

The boy nodded sleepily. 'That'll be great.'

Drew Maxwell patted his shoulder. 'It'll be good to get away from all this fearsome equipment, eh? Have some company—someone to talk to?' Without looking round he held out his hand. Sandie stared at it and a moment later the consultant turned impatiently to her.

'Chart!'

'Oh, yes, of course.' Quickly she snatched it from the end of the bed and handed it to him, a slow flush creeping up her neck. What did he think she was—a thought reader? He glanced down it and handed it back, still without looking at her.

'That's fine,' he told Peter. 'I'm really pleased with you. When you get out of here I hope you're going to give up that motor bike. If it wasn't for your crash helmet you wouldn't be here now, you know.'

The smile melted from the boy's face. 'It wasn't my fault, the accident.'

'I know. That makes it even worse. Have you thought of how little control you have? How much depends on that small metal shell you wear on your head? Save up for a car, Peter. It'll be worth it.'

He walked out of the cubicle, followed by Sandie. 'Of course he'll take no notice,' he muttered, half to himself. 'They never do. The moment he gets out of here he'll forget all he's been through.' He was riffling through the notes in his folder and suddenly he looked at her. 'Devonish. George Devonish?' he frowned.

'Oh, he's this way. In number four,' Sandie said, feeling clever to have remembered the patient's name and position in the ward after only an hour. He glared at her.

'I know where *he* is. It's his notes I can't find,' he snapped. 'Either I left them down in Men's Surgical or my secretary forgot to put them in the folder.' He glanced impatiently round and, seeing no junior nurse on hand, said, 'Oh look, just run down and see if you can find them for me, will you? I'll go on up to Women's Surgical and come back here afterwards to save time.'

Sandie stared at him. 'I—well, I—which floor would it be on?'

But he was half-way down the ward, walking fast. 'Good Lord, Staff!' he flung over his shoulder. 'If I've got to stand and draw you a map I might as well go myself. Surely you can use your head?'

As Sister caught sight of his flying white coat-tail she poked her head anxiously out of the office.

'Everything all right, Mr Maxwell?'

He nodded curtly. 'Just point your staff nurse in the direction of Men's Surgical for me, will you, Sister? She doesn't seem to know where it is.'

'Oh well, she only—' But it was too late. Sister found herself explaining to a pair of swinging doors. She shrugged and turned to Sandie. 'Second floor,' she told her, then went back to Mr Crabtree.

In the lift, Sandie pressed the button for floor two—but when she arrived on Men's Surgical, doctors' rounds were still in progress and sister and staff nurse were fully occupied. She attracted the attention of a young porter and told him what she had come for. He took in the amber-green eyes and tawny hair with appreciation.

'You're new here, aren't you? Haven't seen you before.'

She nodded impatiently. 'Yes, and I'm in a hurry. Do you think you could ask someone whether Mr Maxwell left any notes behind when he was here this morning?'

He drew in his breath sharply. 'Phew, more than

my job's worth. Unless—' He cast a speculative eye over her. 'Unless you made it worth my while. How about having a drink with me tonight, eh? About eight at The Feathers across the road?'

Sandie was about to tell him what she thought of the suggestion when the staff nurse passed hurriedly, going in the direction of Sister's office. She touched her arm.

'Please, I'm sorry to trouble you, but can you tell me whether Mr Maxwell left any notes behind when he was here earlier?'

The other girl looked at her. 'If he did they'll be in the office. Come with me and I'll have a look.'

Sandie followed her into the office and waited while she made a phone call to theatre. The minutes ticked by and she wondered whether the consultant would by now be back on Intensive Care and waiting for her. After what seemed like several hours the staff nurse replaced the receiver and searched through the papers on Sister's desk. Finally she looked up apologetically.

'Sorry, they don't seem to be here. When anyone leaves anything behind Sister always puts it in a prominent place. I should try his office if I were you.'

Sandie turned to go, then hesitated in the doorway, uncertain of which way to turn. The other girl looked at her sympathetically.

'You're new, aren't you? I thought I hadn't seen you before. It's on the ground floor. You'd better ask at the reception desk when you get there.'

Fuming, Sandie got into the lift again and sped groundwards, but when at last she found Drew

Maxwell's office his secretary told her that he had certainly left with notes intact.

He was waiting for her with ill-concealed impatience by the ward doors when she got back to Intensive Care.

'What on earth kept you?' He looked at his watch.

She stared at him. 'I've been searching for the notes you lost—you sent me!'

'I know I did, but I didn't expect it to take this long!'

'I'm afraid I couldn't find them,' she told him breathlessly. 'You don't seem to have left them in either of the places you mentioned.'

'No, I've got them. They were in the folder all the time,' he told her calmly. 'And now, if you don't *mind*, I'd like to examine Mr Devonish. I'm running late this morning as it is!'

Sandie stared after him, speechless with amazement. How thoughtless and inconsiderate could you get? Sister hurried forward to assist, having finished her consultation with Mr Crabtree, leaving Sandie standing in the middle of the ward, completely at a loss. She heard a stifled giggle behind her and turned to see Jenny Sammes, now returned from her break.

'Poor old Sister. She seems scared stiff of Maxie,' she whispered. 'Personally I think he's dreamy.' She rolled her eyes. 'Mmm, I adore the mean, moody and magnificent type, don't you?'

Still smarting, Sandie shrugged. 'Not particularly. I certainly don't think that any man has the right to treat people like slaves just because he happens to be a consultant. I suppose it may have been different in Sister's younger days, but in my last hospital we were treated like human beings!'

Jenny grinned. 'I think he's a bit spoilt. Too used to getting his own way—in this ward, at any rate. I believe Sister has a secret crush on him.' She pulled a face. 'Oh well, I suppose he's more her age than mine, so maybe I'll be generous and let her have him.'

'I pity his poor wife,' Sandie said with feeling.

'Oh, he's not married,' Jenny told her chattily. 'Too dedicated, I suppose He's quite brilliant, you know. I don't suppose any wife would stand for the hours he puts in here.' She gave Sandie a nudge and a saucy wink. 'Maybe it's overwork, combined with a lack of love-life, that makes him so stroppy! Now, I couldn't do much about the overwork, but as for the other—'

'Thank you, Sister. He seems to be making good progress now.' The voice made Sandie jump violently, her cheeks reddening as she realised that Sister and Drew Maxwell had come out of Mr Devonish's cubicle. Could they possibly have overheard Jenny's outrageous remarks? But the consultant gave her only the briefest of glances as he passed on his way out.

When it was time for Sandie to take her lunch-break, Sister suggested that Jenny Sammes should go with her to help her get her bearings. It was a pleasant sunny day and they took a walk round the hospital grounds before going to the nurses' home so that Sandie could unpack a few of her things before going to eat in the canteen. She was delighted with her bright new accommodation, a sunny, spacious room with comfortable furnishings and a neat little shower cubicle adjoining.

'It's miles better than the accommodation at the hospital where I trained,' she told Jenny. 'The rooms there were no bigger than cupboards and the beds were like iron.'

'We're lucky here,' Jenny agreed. 'We have every facility—nice kitchens and laundry rooms—leisure activities too, if you feel like staying around in your time off. It does help, especially if you have a tendency to homesickness.' She perched on the end of the bed. 'Do you have a family? Will you be able to get home on your days off?'

'There's just me and my stepmother now,' Sandie told her. 'My father died six months ago and we moved to Upper Longden, about twelve miles from here, mainly to help us both to settle down.'

'I see. You get along well with your stepmother then?'

'Oh yes.' Sandie pushed the half-empty case under the bed and sat down beside Jenny. 'She's quite young, only about twelve years older than me. I don't remember very much of my own mother. Madeleine's the nearest to a mother I've ever had. We both miss Dad of course, but it hit Maddie particularly hard. I'm hoping I can help her to make a new life here. I've persuaded her to book a holiday in the Caribbean. She's going in a few weeks' time.'

Jenny pulled a face. 'Persuaded! You wouldn't have had to twist *my* arm very hard. Aren't you going too?'

Sandie frowned. 'She wanted me to, but I got this

job and they wanted me to start right away. Besides, I feel she should stand on her own two feet—be independent.'

'Well, I admire your dedication.' Jenny stood up and smoothed down her skirt. 'Oh well, I suppose I'd better be getting back to IC before Sister starts having kittens! Oh, don't leave it too long before you go to the canteen or most of the decent things will be off. See you.' And she whisked out through the door.

Sandie hung up a few more of her things in the wardrobe and unpacked some of her personal possessions—photographs and ornaments—setting them about the room to make it feel more like home. She glanced out of the window at the pleasant view of the garden, thinking wistfully of her father and the pride he took in his own garden at home—the prizes he used to win for his begonias. Suddenly she looked at her watch and was shocked to find that she had already used almost half of her break. She was hungry, too. She'd never last until this evening without a bite to eat. Stowing the now empty case in the cupboard over the wardrobe, she locked her door and ran down the stairs. On the steps outside she paused, trying to remember the geography of the place. Yes, Jenny had said the canteen was that way, round the corner of the nurses' home and towards the back of the hospital. She'd better get a move on if she was to get anything to eat at all.

The thought of food uppermost in her mind, she ran round the corner of the building and cannoned straight into someone coming in the opposite direction. The impact knocked the breath from her body and as she staggered back against the wall two hands grasped her by the elbows.

'Good heavens! Are you all right?'

'Yes, I think so! I'm sorry, I—oh!' She looked up and found herself looking into Drew Maxwell's astonished face.

'That'll teach me to take a short cut to the car park!' He looked vaguely amused. 'Where's the fire? I thought nurses were only supposed to run in an emergency.'

'I was just going to the canteen for lunch,' she said lamely, her cheeks crimson.

'Really? The cuisine must have improve dramatically since the last time I ate there!' he remarked.

He let go her elbows and she lifted her hands to straighten her cap. 'I've been unpacking and I didn't notice the time,' she told him.

'Ah, yes, that reminds me. I believe I owe you an apology. Until Sister Milton told me, I wasn't aware that this was your first day at Hartmoor. I wouldn't have sent you on that errand if I'd known.'

She shrugged. 'It's all right. I had to get to know the lay-out of the hospital some time.' She glanced up at him. 'Though I would have preferred to do it in my own time.' Her look was rewarded with the smile she had seen him give his patient earlier this morning; the smile that lifted the corners of the long, mobile mouth and crinkled the corners of his eyes.

'And for something more useful than a wild goose chase, eh?' he supplied. 'I shall try to be more careful in future, Nurse—Masters, isn't it?' He raised an eyebrow. 'And you may be gratified to know that my secretary was very cross with me for the implication that *she* was less than efficient!' He patted her shoulder. 'And now, if you're going to get that lunch you're so hungry for, you'd better run along.'

He walked away in the direction of the car park and Sandie stared after him. *Run along!* Did he have to spoil everything by treating her like an errant schoolgirl? It was true he had had the grace to apologise, but in such a patronising way! Maybe she hadn't been all that wrong about him after all . . .

That evening when they both came off duty, Jenny Sammes suggested that they share a meal. Sandie hadn't yet had time to shop for food and Jenny seemed to have ample for two in her corner of the fridge.

'You'll have to be careful about marking everything,' she advised as she took out bacon, eggs and sausages. 'There are some people here who are only too glad of an excuse to nick your last egg.' She waved a bottle of milk. 'Do you fancy a coffee while you're waiting?'

Sandie nodded eagerly. 'I'd love one. I'll make it, shall I?' She sniffed appreciatively at the aroma of frying bacon. 'Mmm—that smells good! I only had time for a sandwich at lunch-time and I'm ravenous.'

Jenny looked up. 'Oh, what did you use the rest of the time for then? Settling in?'

Sandie gave her a wry smile. 'I managed to spend most of it running into Mr Maxwell—literally, I mean. I was on my way to the canteen, not looking where I was going, and I ran smack into him. It was very embarrassing.'

Jenny winced. 'Ouch! Still, serves him right for making you run all over the hospital for nothing this morning.'

'He apologised for that,' Sandie admitted. 'Though he did it in a patronising way. It seems that Sister Milton told him it was my first day here. He ended the conversation by telling me to "run along" as though I was about five years old.'

Jenny nodded sympathetically, giving the bacon a vicious prod.

They had just finished eating when there was a tap on the door and a girl looked in to tell Sandie that she was wanted on the telephone. She went out into the corridor and found that it was Madeleine, her stepmother, calling.

'I've been thinking of you all day, wondering how you were getting on. Have you had a good day?'

'Fine,' Sandie told her. 'It's all a bit strange at first of course, much bigger than I'm used to, but the nurses' home is lovely. I'll soon settle down, don't worry. How are you?'

There was a small silence at the other end of the line. 'I'm fine too. There's a lot to do in the house as you know. I'm missing you though. Will you be able to get home at the weekend?'

Sandie hesitated. 'I could, I suppose, but I had intended to stay here. It's time you started to make a new life for yourself, Maddie. Why don't you get out and join something—meet some new people? After all, that's why we moved, to make a fresh start.'

'It isn't that easy,' Madeleine said painfully. 'I

was married to James for eight years and in all that time we only needed each other. I still feel I'm only half a person.'

Sandie's throat tightened. 'I know, I know. But you're still young, Maddie. It's such a waste. Dad wouldn't have wanted you to be like this.'

There was a pause, then, 'Sandie, if I invite a few of the local people in for a drink on Sunday morning after church, will you come home and help me to entertain them?'

'Of course I will! That's a super idea. I'll see you on Saturday then. Bye for now, Maddie.' Sandie gave a sigh of relief as she replaced the receiver. If only she could get her stepmother to make some new friends she would be all right, she was sure.

Elm Court, the small Cotswold stone house that Madeleine Masters had bought after her husband's death, was in Upper Longden, a delightful village that looked as though it had slipped out of a bygone age, with its quaint stone cottages, its leafy lanes and tiny shops. Ducks drowsed round the edges of the pond opposite the twelfth-century church and the neat cottage gardens were fragrant with all the old-fashioned flowers. It was a far cry from the industrial Midlands town where Sandie had been born, but she had loved it on sight. When she arrived on Saturday, just after lunch, she found that her stepmother had been busy during the week. Decorators had transformed the hall and drawing-room from their former gloom to a bright new freshness. Madeleine had been to a sale and had bought one or two interesting pieces of antique furniture. She had also been busy making new curtains. Sandie stood looking around appreciatively.

'You've done wonders in just one week, Maddie!' she exclaimed. 'I wouldn't have believed it!'

'The carpets were only laid yesterday. I was terrified in case it wouldn't be finished in time for Sunday,' Madeleine told her. 'But apart from that, I wanted to get as much as I could done before my holiday. Next week they're coming to refit the kitchen and bathroom.'

Sandie gave her stepmother a hug. 'I'm glad you've been keeping busy. You do like it here, don't you, Maddie? You really are enjoying doing the house up?'

Madeleine smiled. 'Of course I am. Just give me time, darling. I'll be fine. Now, I've made some things for the party and put them in the freezer. Just some little snacks. Come and see.'

The following morning Madeleine went to church. Sandie decided not to accompany her, but to stay behind and get everything ready for the party which was to follow the service. She quite enjoyed herself as she went between kitchen and drawing-room with trays laden with plates and glasses.

The house really was shaping well. When she had first seen it she hadn't liked it at all, but Madeleine had seen its potential and now she was proving herself right with her flair for decor and furnishing. The pine panelling in the hall had been stripped of its accumulation of dark vanish and now gleamed like creamy satin, set off warmly by the new rose-pink carpet and softly shaded wall lights. In the drawing-room, wine-coloured velvet curtains hung at the long windows, their affect jewel-like against white walls and carpet. A wood fire burned in the stone fireplace and there were flowers everywhere; Madeleine had always been brilliant at arranging them.

At twelve o'clock Sandie took a last look round and decided to slip upstairs and change. She chose a black skirt and soft blue blouse with a pretty frilled collar. Unpinning her hair from its usual coil, she brushed it out around her shoulders and made up her face carefully. She hadn't yet met any of the local people and she wanted to make a good impression for Madeleine's sake. She was just taking a last look in the mirror when she heard the front door slam.

'Sandie! I'm home. Are you coming down?' Madeleine called up the stairs.

Madeleine stood in the hall looking nervous. She smiled at Sandie. 'Thank you, darling, you've made everything look so nice. You look pretty, too. I've poured out some sherries ready. Will you give me a hand with them? The first guests will be here at any minute.'

Sandie squeezed her arm reassuringly. 'Of course, and don't worry. They're only ordinary people.'

In the kitchen Madeleine sneaked a look into the mirror, tucking in a stray strand of her dark hair, her brown eyes wide with anxiety. 'Oh dear, I wonder if they'll all come? I saw most of them at church—all, in fact, except the man at Snow House. He wasn't there when I called, either, so I just dropped the invitation in. I do hope he won't think it a cheek when we haven't met properly.'

The doorbell rang and Sandie touched her step-mother's arm. 'Don't worry, I'll get it. And I wouldn't worry about that man. If he doesn't come you'll probably find you're better off without him!'

The guests began to arrive quickly after that. There were the vicar and his wife; Andrew Phillips, the local GP, the village schoolmistress and about a dozen others. Sandie was kept busy refilling glasses and making small talk. She was just passing Madeleine, who was standing by the window talk-ing to the vicar, when she heard her stepmother give a muffled exclamation.

'Oh dear! Sandie—' Sandie turned. 'It's the man from Snow House. He's just coming up the drive. Go and let him in, dear, will you?'

Sandie stood looking for somewhere to put her tray down. There were still three full glasses on it, but every available surface seemed to be full of plates. She heard the insistent peal of the doorbell and Madeleine shot her an anxious glance over the vicar's shoulder.

In the hall Sandie put the tray down on the table and opened the heavy front door.

'Good morning. I hope this is all right, just coming. I intended to telephone you and—Oh! It's you!'

Sandie looked up to find herself staring into the surpised grey eyes of Drew Maxwell. 'No!' she said, blushing furiously. 'It isn't me—I mean, it wasn't me who invited you.'

He frowned. 'You didn't? But I—'

'It was my stepmother,' Sandie put in quickly. 'She lives here. It's her party.' She bit her lip hard, angry at her gauche behaviour. She was stammering like a fool. What must he think of her? She held the door wide and stepped back.

'Come in, please,' she urged. 'Madeleine will be so pleased that you were able to come after all.' She glanced round and her eye caught the tray of drinks. At least she could redeem herself by offering him one. 'Have a sherry.'

She seized the tray and spun round with it, but unfortunately he was standing too close to her and the tray struck his elbow. The three full glasses teetered precariously across the slippery surface and before Sandie's horrified eyes they toppled over, cascading their sticky brown contents down the front of Drew Maxwell's expensive, handwoven tweed jacket!

CHAPTER TWO

SANDIE froze with horror. It was as though the whole thing was happening in slow motion. One minute she had been about to offer him a drink and the next she was watching the dark stain spreading on his jacket. She looked up at him disbelievingly. She was dreaming this, she *had* to be! But the answering look in his eyes was all too real and a moment later Madeleine's horrified exclamation brought her to her senses.

'*Sandie!* Oh dear.' She had been coming out into the hall to greet her late guest just as the accident had happened. 'Run and get a cloth, Sandie.' She looked at Drew. 'Perhaps if you took it off? Sandie will take it to the kitchen and sponge it for you, won't you, dear? I'm so sorry.'

Drew took off the jacket, revealing a cream polo-neck sweater, and handed it to Sandie, who escaped gratefully to the kitchen without another word. Once there she spread the garment on the table and looked at it. It was really good material so warm water and a clean cloth should do the trick, she told herself. Finding the cloth, she set to work, trying hard not to let her mind dwell on the man who owned the jacket or what he must be thinking about her at this moment. When she had finished she slipped the garment over the back of a chair and put it close to the radiator to dry, then she sat down and poured herself a generous measure of sherry

24

from the bottle on the table. She had just raised it to her lips and taken a comforting sip when the door opened.

'I thought you might like to know that none of the glasses were broken.'

Sandie stared at the man standing in the doorway, tray in hand. His lips twitched with amusement.

'Oh dear! Have I discovered your secret vice or are you just reviving yourself?' He came in and closed the door, putting the tray of empty glasses down on the table. Sandie jumped to her feet and moved behind the chair in an unconsciously defensive gesture.

'Your jacket will soon be dry. I think the stain has come out. If not, you must send it to the cleaners and let me have the bill.'

'Well, that's an improvement,' he said, his eyes glittering with laughter.

She looked at him. 'Improvement? I don't see—' She stopped, noticing for the first time that he was having trouble keeping the corners of his mouth from lifting.

'I thought out there in the hall that the accident had rendered you speechless!'

She blushed. 'Oh, I haven't really apologised, have I? I'm sorry.'

He took a step closer. 'I didn't mean that at all. Come now, it's not so terrible.' He looked at the hands that clutched the back of the chair. 'You don't have to protect yourself against me, you know. At this moment you look rather like a lady lion-tamer about to go into action. Please, sit down and finish your sherry.'

She bit her lip. His tolerant attitude was, if anything, more intimidating than his anger might have been. What did he find so amusing about having sherry poured down his jacket? She looked down at his legs.

'Are your trousers all right?'

He looked down, then up at her face with an expression of surprise. 'I believe so. Why?'

She blushed hotly. 'I meant did any of the sherry get on to them?'

He smiled. 'No, though I believe there are a few spots on your stepmother's new carpet.'

Sandie groaned and sat down heavily on the chair. 'Oh no! Whatever is the matter with me? I'm not usually so clumsy.'

He laughed, a deep throaty chuckle that Sandie would ordinarily have found infectious. As it was, she was unable to meet his gaze until he said quite suddenly, 'Do you like horses?'

She looked up, her eyes widening. 'Yes, I love them. Why?'

'Then come and see mine this afternoon. It's Snow House, about half a mile down the lane. Come at half-past two—right?'

She nodded dumbly and he patted her arm. 'That's settled then. You can bring the jacket with you when you come. I'll see you later.'

When he had gone she drank the rest of her sherry in one gulp. She had behaved like an absolute idiot—stammering and nodding. Perhaps he had felt sorry for her! She went across to the jacket and examined it. Thank goodness the stain seemed to have vanished. At least she had managed to do that without bungling it!

Madeleine was sympathetic and did her best to comfort her. 'He didn't seem at all cross to me,' she said reassuringly. 'Anyway, I'm sure that a man in his position must have whole wardrobes full of clothes. I hear he's a consultant neurosurgeon, quite an eminent one.'

Sandie nodded. 'Yes, he's at Hartmoor General.'

'Oh, you mean you know him! You actually work together?' Madeleine asked.

Sandie reached up to the cupboard with the last of the glasses she had been drying. 'I'd hardly say we worked *together*. I think he sees nurses as lesser mortals!'

'I'm sure that isn't true.' Madeleine smiled reminiscently. 'He's quite devastatingly attractive, isn't he? That fascinating streak of silver hair, and he has such a vibrant personality.'

Sandie hung up her tea-towel thoughtfully. 'As a matter of fact, he's invited me to go and see his horses this afternoon, at half-past two.'

Madeleine beamed. 'There! What did I tell you?' She looked at her watch. 'Half-past two! In that case we'd better have lunch at once. You won't want to be late!'

Snow House was delightful. It was built of centuries old Cotswold stone with tall, straight chimneys and a multitude of dormer windows. The mullioned, lattice-paned casements glittered in the afternoon sunshine and as Sandie waited for her ring at the front door bell to be answered she admired a group of ancient chestnut trees just coming into luxuriant blossom by the gate. She had changed into her jeans and a sweater, hoping that perhaps Drew would invite her to ride. It was ages since she had been on a horse, not since she had begun her nursing training, and she felt quite excited at the prospect.

Drew opened the door to her himself. He, too, had changed into riding gear. He invited her in.

'Mrs Bradshaw, my housekeeper, has her afternoon off on a Sunday,' he explained as he led her through the wide hall. 'She goes to see her sister in Tewkesbury. As a matter of fact, I rather like having the house to myself.' He opened a side door. 'The stables are out here. Shall we go out?'

Sandie was suddenly aware of the dress bag she carried, into which she had carefully packed the jacket. 'Oh, I'd better give this to you before anything else happens to it,' she told him, handing it over.

He put it on a chair by the door. 'Thank you. I'll hang it up later.'

The door gave on to a small stable yard with two loose boxes. Both half-doors were open at the top and as Drew and Sandie came out, two heads appeared, nostrils flaring and ears pricked forward expectantly. Drew whistled and both animals whinnied excitedly.

'Oh, they're beautiful!' Sandie exclaimed. She had slipped a few sugar lumps into her pocket and she took them out, glancing first at Drew for approval. 'May I?'

He nodded with a smile. 'You'll be their devoted friend for life.'

She fed them the sugar and stroked the nuzzling, velvet noses, first the little mare with the pretty white face, then the handsome gelding with the flying chestnut mane.

'What are their names?' she asked.

'The gelding is Fagin, because in spite of his innocent look he's a terrible pick-pocket, and the little mare is Sheila.' He looked down at Sandie's long, slim, demin-clad legs. 'Perhaps you'd like to ride. Do you have a hard hat and a pair of boots?'

Sandie shook her head regretfully. 'Not any more. I haven't ridden regularly since I was at school. But I'm sure I can manage without.'

He shook his head gravely. 'Not on my horses. I've seen too many head injuries to allow anyone to risk that. But never mind. I think I can fix you up. Come and look at the garden first. I think you'll like it.' He led the way through a small hand gate and she followed him, a little mystified.

Why was he treating her like this? Did he feel obliged to entertain her because Madeleine was his new neighbour? Did he feel that she needed humouring in some way?

As she passed through the gate in front of him she suddenly knew what Madeleine had meant when she called him vibrant. There was a powerful aura of strength about him; the broad shoulders, the proud set of his head and the strong, hard bones of his face. Sandie looked away, her cheeks warming as she was suddenly very much aware of him as a man. As the sun shone on his hair it picked out the silver highlights and the fascinating streak that sprang back from his brow. As though her eyes drew his, he turned to look at her.

'Quite a view, don't you think?' He nodded towards the garden that fell away from them in a series of natural terraces to blend with the sweep of the valley beyond, a patchwork of greens, gold and browns. She caught her breath.

'Oh, it's beautiful! I'm beginning to see now why Madeleine wanted to come and live in the Cotswolds. She was always trying to persuade my father to come after he retired, but he would never leave the Midlands where he was born.'

He looked at her. 'I hadn't realised until today that you were Mrs Masters' stepdaughter. You must miss your father very much.'

'Yes, I do.'

He walked on, leading her through the garden, obviously fashioned many years before. It was a fascinating maze of stone-walled walks; flights of steep steps gave on to little paved terraces, edged with rock plants. And in the centre of it all was a lawn fringed by yew trees cut into fantastic shapes. In the centre of this was a large, oblong pool, the surface of which was covered with water lilies.

'I understand that this was once a trout pool,' he told her. 'It seems that many houses had them at one time—for gastronomic use, of course.'

She gazed at it in awe. 'Really? It's so large— much too big for a lily pool.'

He chuckled. 'Yes. I like to imagine the Regency bucks diving into it to sober up after their all-night card parties.' He took her arm. 'Come on, let's go and see if we can find you a hat and some boots.'

She waited at the stables while he went into the house, reappearing a few minutes later with a hat and boots which fitted perfectly. As she put them on she wondered briefly who they belonged to.

By the time she was ready Drew had saddled the

horses up. He led out the mare and cupped his hands to help Sandie mount, but she shook her head. Somehow it seemed sacrilegious to put her booted foot into the hands of a consultant surgeon.

'I think I can manage, thanks.'

Drew watched admiringly as she swung herself into the saddle. 'Well done!' He smiled up at her and her heart gave a sudden lurch. Madeleine was right, he *was* attractive.

They rode in silence, walking until they turned off the road and on to a bridle path, then trotting until they reached open country, after which Drew pressed his heels into the gelding's flanks and leapt ahead. Sandie followed, exhilarated to find that the riding skills she had learned years ago had not deserted her. The mare was fit and full of spirit as she followed the gelding across the fields, her dainty hoofs thudding on the soft ground, and Sandie's heart sang with the joy and freedom of it. At last they stopped under a clump of trees close to a stream. Drew dismounted and held her reins for her.

'Here, let me help you.' She swung her legs over the saddle and he held out his arms and caught her by the waist as she slid down. As her feet touched the ground she was momentarily pressed against him and the breath caught in her throat. He smelt of expensive tweed, leather and warm male skin. She felt her pulses race as she lifted her face to look up at him. He was smiling.

'You ride well, Sandie. By the way, what is that short for?'

She threw herself down on the grass at the stream's edge, pulling off the borrowed hard hat.

'Alexandra, would you believe? Awful, isn't it? I really enjoyed that gallop, but I bet I'll be as stiff as a post tomorrow!'

He lowered himself beside her. 'If you haven't ridden for some time, I expect you will be. But that shouldn't bother someone of your age.'

'I'm almost twenty-two!' she said, lifting her head sharply.

He laughed. 'Oh dear! Do forgive me. I must say that you're wearing extremely well for one of such advanced years!'

She coloured painfully as she saw that he was laughing at her again. It was odd, she reflected. She had done more blushing today than ever before in her life!

'Tell me a little about yourself,' he said. 'Did you go to school in the Midlands?'

'No. I went to a convent in Hampshire,' she told him. 'My parents had me rather late in life. I was their only child and I think they thought I should get used to being independent as soon as possible. They sent me away to school when I was eight.'

He looked thoughtful. 'That was a very unselfish thing for them to do. It must have been a great sacrifice.'

She nodded. 'Yes, especially as my mother died only two years later. Dad married Madeleine four years after that, just before he retired. She was always trying to get him to come and live here in the Cotswolds, but he said he was too set in his ways.'

Drew smiled. 'Not too set to marry an attractive young wife!' He looked at Sandie. 'And how did the two of you take to each other?'

'Very well. Maddie would have liked me to come

home and go to school locally after she and Dad were married,' she told him. 'She said I'd become institutionalised. She used to tell me I wasn't house-trained!' Sandie laughed. 'After this morning you probably go along with that opinion!'

He looked suddenly serious. 'Do I seem forbidding to you?'

She was taken aback by the question. 'No, of course not,' she said, too quickly. 'At least, not today.' Her eyes slid away from his. 'Thank you for being so understanding about the sherry and for asking me here this afternoon. It was very kind of you.'

He smiled indulgently. 'What a polite child!' He saw the denial on her lips and put out a finger to stop it. 'No, don't say it. Don't destroy the illusion. One day you'll be sorry you were so quick to deny your youth. It slips away all too soon, you know.'

'Anyone would think you were ninety!' The words were out before she could stop them and she caught her lower lip between her teeth, horrified at the familiarity. To her surprise he laughed, the same infectious chuckle she had heard already once today. Getting to his feet he took her hand and pulled her up, too.

'Time I took you home. That stepmother of yours will be wondering what I've done with you.'

She looked at her watch, amazed to find that it was almost five o'clock. 'Heavens! I suppose I should be getting back, though Maddie is so busy with the house I don't suppose she will have even missed me.' She made to mount the mare but he bent to pick something up from the grass.

'Wait, you're forgetting this.' She turned and he

put the hat on for her, fastening it under the chin. His fingers were firm and warm against the cool skin of her cheek and she looked up at him, her heart quickening a little at his proximity and the intimacy of the gesture. His hand cupped her chin.

'Will you have dinner with me one evening?' he asked quietly.

Her eyes widened. Had she heard correctly? 'I—yes,' she said breathlessly, swallowing hard.

The corners of his mouth twitched; then suddenly, without warning, he bent and kissed her. It was a hard, uncompromising kiss and somehow she knew it hadn't been an impulsive gesture. Drew Maxwell was not a man of impulse.

He let her go abruptly and mounted his horse, swinging the animal's head round towards home. 'Hurry up!' he called as he moved away. 'There might just be time for a quick cup of tea if you hurry.'

Swiftly she hauled herself into the saddle and urged the little mare after him, his kiss still stinging her lips. As she watched the tall, straight figure riding ahead of her, it suddenly occurred to her that he wore no hat. Was that a significant facet of his nature? Was there one set of rules for him and another for everyone else? Was he so arrogant that he thought of himself as indestructible? Was she supposed to consider herself highly honoured, being asked out to dinner by him? She cringed inwardly at the naive way she had accepted. Half closing her eyes she saw again his expression as he had fastened on her hat, felt the tingling pressure of his lips on hers and knew that, come what may, she had to find out more about him.

At the stables she took off her hat and changed the boots for her own shoes while Drew unsaddled the horses. As she looked inside that hat she noticed a name-tape with the name *Anita Banks*, and wondered briefly who she could be. Obviously someone Drew knew well and who was in the habit of staying with him here at Snow House. Deep inside she felt a pang of something. Jealousy? Sandie thrust the thought aside, smoothing back her dishevelled hair. What an idea! What was there to be jealous of?

She refused his offer of tea and when he offered to take her home in his car she shook her head. 'It's so near. I can easily walk. Maybe it'll help to loosen up my muscles a little.'

He walked with her as far as the gate. 'About that dinner,' he began. She turned to him.

'I forgot—I'll be on nights for the next few days.'

His eyes clouded. 'I see. In that case perhaps we'd better leave it for the time being. I'll see you again. Goodbye, Sandie.'

As she walked home she felt deflated. Had he regretted asking her out and seized on the opportunity to let it slide? Did he hope that she'd forget he'd mentioned it in the first place?'

When she came in Madeleine looked searchingly at her. 'Well, did you have a nice time?'

Sandie threw herself down into a chair. 'Yes, but I bet I'm going to be as stiff as a post tomorrow. The horses were lovely but it's so long since I rode. Snow House is a dream and—' She stopped speaking as she looked up and saw Madeleine's expression.

'You like him rather a lot, don't you?' her step-mother asked perceptively.

Sandie coloured. 'He's nicer than I thought at first. When I met him on my first day at Hartmoor he seemed bad-tempered and quite rude.'

Madeleine smiled wryly. 'A man as attractive as he is must need some sort of defence mechanism with all those adoring young women around.'

Sandie stood up and stretched her already stiff-ening limbs. 'You've been watching too many of those soap operas, Maddie. Hospital life isn't really like that at all, you know.'

Madeleine drew the corners of her mouth down. 'No, of course not.' She glanced cautiously up at her stepdaughter. 'Are you seeing him again?'

'I can hardly help it under the circumstances, can I?' Sandie said evasively.

'I see. He hasn't invited you out then?'

Sandie walked over to the window, biting her lip at the memory of her inept refusal of Drew's invi-tation. 'As a matter of fact he did,' she admitted. 'But as I'm going to be on nights next week I had to say no.'

'Oh, what a shame. But surely he'll ask you again?' Madeleine suggested sympathetically.

Sandie shrugged. 'Perhaps.' She turned towards the door. 'I'd better go up and have that bath before my poor joints seize up altogether.' But as she reached the doorway she paused. 'Maddie, have you heard the name Anita Banks since you've been here?'

Madeleine looked up. 'Yes, but long before we came here to live. Why do you ask?'

'Drew Maxwell lent me a riding hat and a pair of

boots this afternoon. That was the name inside them. Who is she?'

'Surely you've heard of her? She's a model,' Madeleine told her. 'Quite a successful one. You can hardly pick up one of the glossies without seeing her face.' She frowned. 'Do you think she's a regular visitor at Snow House, then?'

'She must be, mustn't she, if she leaves a set of riding gear there?' Sandie tried to make her voice light as she called the words over her shoulder on her way to the stairs. Anita Banks must be Drew Maxwell's girlfriend—or even his fiancée. But if he were engaged to a glamorous model, what was he doing asking a mere staff nurse out to dinner? Inviting her to ride his precious horses—*kissing* her? The answer was painfully obvious. She had simply been an amusing way of passing a rather dull Sunday afternoon!

CHAPTER THREE

NIGHT DUTY on Intensive Care proved uneventful. There were no new emergency cases and Sandie found plenty of time for her own thoughts as she made the routine two-hourly rounds, taking blood samples and making temperature, pulse and respiration checks. She didn't see Drew once during the time and quite convinced herself that he had forgotten all about the Sunday afternoon they spent together. Jenny had been transferred to another ward but they met occasionally in the corridor and one afternoon as Sandie was getting up the other girl knocked on her door.

'Hi!' she said brightly. 'I thought I'd come and see how you were getting on. I've been on early duty and I've just come off. Fancy having something to eat with me? I couldn't face the canteen.'

Sandie smiled. 'Come in. It'd be nice to have a chat. Being on nights so soon after starting here hasn't given me much chance of getting to know people and I'm feeling a bit remote from everything.'

The other girl looked sympathetic. 'Poor you. I should have thought of that. When you come off nights I'll take you round and introduce you to some of the others.'

'How's your new ward?' Sandie asked her.

'Women's Surgical?' Jenny pulled a face. 'It would be quite interesting if it weren't for Sister

Scraggs. Milton is a positive angel compared to her!'

'Difficult, is she?'

Jenny raised her eyes ceiling-wards. 'You can say that again! One of the old school—all starch. The only advantage is that you can always hear her coming. She sounds like someone doing the Highland Fling in a bath of cornflakes! I'll swear she even starches her knickers!'

They giggled together over eggs and bacon in the kitchen and Sandie felt cheered. Although Jenny chattered on about her friends and her medical student boyfriend, Sandie did not respond by telling her about her afternoon with Drew Maxwell. Somehow she felt instinctively that he wouldn't want it known that he had entertained a staff nurse for the afternoon. Besides that, she was now quite sure that his invitation to dinner had been a whim that would never be fulfilled. She did, however, tell Jenny about Madeleine's drinks party and the incident with the sherry. Jenny spluttered over her coffee.

'Oh God, how awful! You must have wished the floor would open and swallow you up! What happened? Was he absolutely livid?'

'No, he was quite nice about it actually. I did manage to get the stain out for him,' Sandie said.

'Well now!' Jenny raised an eyebrow. 'Nice to you, eh? Next thing we know he'll be asking you for a date. That'd make a few people sit up and take notice!' She laughed. 'He's made a few hearts round here flutter, I can tell you, but then that's always the way with the enigmatic type, isn't it? There are always speculation and rumours in a hospital and what people can't find out, they make up. By the way, I've never asked you if you have a boyfriend.' She leaned forward eagerly. 'Is there someone back in the Midlands eating his heart out for you?'

'I shouldn't think so.' Sandie was glad to get the subject off Drew. 'I was going out with someone for a while, but that ended some time ago and I was too busy studying for my finals after that.'

Jenny sat up suddenly. 'Why did you have to go and utter that dirty word, *finals*? I've got a pile of books waiting in my room and I haven't the slightest inclination to open one of them! But I must.' She got up from the table. 'Shall we do the washing-up?'

'I'll do it,' Sandie offered. 'You go and have an hour with those books. I always found that little and often was the way when it came to studying.'

Jenny groaned and stretched. 'Oooh, you don't know how lucky you are, having all that over and done with. Still, this time next year—' She grinned at Sandie. 'Well, if you're really sure about the washing-up, I think I'll take your advice. Bye.'

As she washed the dishes, Sandie reflected that her instinct had been right. If rumour got around about her and Drew Maxwell, she could become unpopular, especially in view of the short time she had been here at Hartmoor General.

She was relieved when her stint on nights came to an end and she could take her break. She telephoned Madeleine to say she would be home and was concerned to detect a depressed note in her stepmother's voice.

'I've missed you so much, Sandie. It'll be nice to

have some life about the place.' She sighed. 'You know, I'm beginning to think I'd have been better off with a flat in town instead of buying Elm Court. It really can be very lonely here.'

'Oh dear, haven't you made any friends yet?' Sandie asked.

'Not really, but perhaps that's because I've been so busy. I'm certainly not short of something to occupy me. You'll see quite a difference in the house when you come home this time, Sandie. Oh, it will be lovely to have you here for a few days.'

When she arrived at Elm Court, Sandie saw that Madeleine hadn't exaggerated. The new bathroom was finished and Madeleine's bedroom had been decorated and refurnished in pretty shades of pink and grey. She showed it to her stepdaughter with pride.

'I've been sleeping in your room while it was done,' she said. 'Yours is next on the list.' She sighed wearily. 'Do you know, I shall be quite glad to leave for my holiday after all. All this has been much harder work than I expected. And another thing I hadn't taken into account is the garden. It's too large for me to manage on my own and so far I haven't found a suitable gardener.'

Sandie looked at her pale face and the tell-tale shadows under her eyes. 'Why don't you leave the rest of it until you've had your holiday?' she suggested. 'Do something more interesting— like giving a dinner party, for instance. I'd help you.'

Madeleine squeezed her arm. 'I know you would. But you should be living your own life. I realise it can't be easy for you either. Leaving all your friends behind to come here with me must have been hard for you. Now tell me what you've been doing since you were home last. Have you been out? Have you seen anything of the dashing Mr Maxwell?'

Sandie laughed and shook her head. 'I've been on nights, remember? I haven't seen much of anyone, except the patients—and intensive care patients are hardly in a position to be sociable, even at the best of times!'

Madeleine shook her head. 'Poor Sandie.'

'Oh, I'm not complaining,' Sandie said quickly. 'I love the work. I just haven't had much chance to make friends yet at Hartmoor.'

Madeleine looked thoughtful. 'Maybe a dinner party would be a good idea for both of us. Who should we ask?'

Sandie shrugged. 'Some of the people you asked to drinks the other Sunday, I suppose. The ones you liked best.'

Upstairs in her room she unpacked her case, then went and had a bath in the new bathroom. Afterwards she changed into black velvet jeans and a white angora sweater, brushing out her hair loosely. It was nice to dress in something soft and feminine. For the past few days she seemed to have lived either in her uniform or a dressing-gown, except on the occasions that she had hurriedly dressed to run out to the shops.

Just as she reached the foot of the stairs the doorbell rang and as Madeleine didn't seem to be anywhere around she went to answer it. To her surprise, Drew Maxwell stood on the step. Her eyes widened.

'Oh! Hallo.' For a moment they stood, staring at each other, then she said, 'Well, er, what can I do for you?'

He looked amused. 'As a matter of fact I was invited to a pre-dinner drink. Your stepmother invited me. She rang a little while ago and said she wanted to consult me about something.'

Sandie bit her lip. 'Oh, I'm so sorry! Please come in.' She led him through to the drawing-room and offered him a chair. Snatching up the cigarette box from the coffee table she opened it and handed it to him. He shook his head.

'No, thank you. I don't seem to have seen you around lately.'

She replaced the box. 'No, I've been on nights.'

'Of course. I remember now, you told me.'

She racked her brain to think of something sparkling and intelligent to say while he looked expectantly at her.

'Have you—' she began, but at that moment the door opened and Madeleine came in. She looked a little surprised when she saw Drew.

'Oh, Sandie, you should have told me that Mr Maxwell had arrived. How rude you must have thought me.' She held out her hand to Drew. 'How nice of you to come at such short notice, Mr Maxwell. What will you drink? I believe I remember that you like whisky and soda. Am I right?'

He smiled. 'You are—and please, call me Drew.' He took the drink from Madeleine and sat down, looking relaxed. Sandie wished that she had Maddie's ease of manner.

'Before I forget, I'm giving a little dinner party

quite soon,' Madeleine told him. 'I do hope you'll come.' She glanced at him out of the corner of her eye. 'I have, er, heard that a certain—celebrity comes to stay at Snow House occasionally. I wondered if you would like to bring her with you?'

Sandie stared at her stepmother, feeling the warm colour spreading up from her neck. What was she thinking of? Drew would know for sure that Sandie was the only person who could have told her about Anita Banks! She buried her face in her glass, not daring to look at him as she heard him say,

'You must mean Anita. Well, thank you. I'd love to come and I'm sure she would too if it happened to coincide with one of her visits. She doesn't manage to get down very often, being so busy, but if you can possibly let me have the date in good time I'll contact her and see what can be done.'

Sandie wanted to run away and hide, but she remained rooted to the spot as she heard her stepmother continue, 'Are you—I mean, may we expect a local wedding in the near future?'

Sandie risked a quick look in Drew's direction and saw that he was looking somewhat mystified.

'As far as I know, Anita has no plans to marry at present,' he said. 'Have I missed something in the gossip columns?' He looked from Madeleine to Sandie and back again. 'I—take it that you were referring to Anita?'

'I—yes, I rather thought—' Madeleine blushed as she fumbled for words.

'My sister's career seems to fill her entire life at the moment.' Sandie saw a sudden flash of realisation cross his face as the situation became clear to him. 'Ah! Perhaps you didn't understand that Anita was my sister?' he said.

Madeleine bit her lip. 'I, er—well, of course it makes no difference. We shall be delighted to meet her. You must certainly bring her if she is at home at the time.' She cleared her throat. 'And now I must ask you if you could help me with another matter. Do you know of a good gardener who is looking for work? I really do need one desperately.'

When Drew left a short time later Sandie walked out on to the drive with him. Feeling that some explanation was due she said awkwardly,

'I'm sorry about the misunderstanding. I'm afraid my stepmother rather jumped to the wrong conclusion.' She couldn't stop herself blushing as she said it, knowing that Madeleine wasn't the only one who had assumed that Anita Banks was romantically connected with him.

He smiled. 'Please don't worry about it.'

She shook her head. 'I feel I must explain. You must be wondering—' He laid a hand on her arm and smiled into her eyes.

'Save it for tomorrow evening, at dinner. That is, if you're free.' He looked enquiringly at her and she stared back, tongue-tied. 'I did ask you before and you seemed to find the idea quite agreeable then,' he reminded her. 'But perhaps you've forgotten.'

'Oh no!' She found her voice. 'That is, I'd love to come—thank you.'

He got into his car and smiled at her through the open window. 'Good. I'll pick you up here at about eight. Will that be all right?'

'Yes, that will be fine.' She stood looking after

the car as it swept down the drive. Why couldn't she react like girls in books, all cool sophistication and mysterious smiles? Every time he spoke to her she was either tongue-tied or too quick to say the wrong thing! Had he asked her out to dinner because he really wanted to, or because he felt sorry for her?

She went back to the drawing-room to find Madeleine waiting for her, her face anguished.

'Oh dear, I've never been so embarrassed in my life! How could I have been so stupid?' She poured herself another sherry and sipped it gratefully, glancing at Sandie as she did so. 'I'm sorry, darling. Have I made things impossible for you?'

Sandie smiled at her, feeling suddenly light-hearted. 'No. As a matter of fact, it's quite the opposite!'

But Madeleine was still smarting at the memory of her *faux pas*. 'I really don't think I can face him again. Not for some time, anyway,' she muttered. 'But then I don't suppose I shall have to!'

'That's where you're wrong,' Sandie told her. 'He'll be round again tomorrow evening.'

Madeleine looked up at her. 'He will? Oh, you mean?'

'Yes. He's asked me out to dinner. And this time I've said yes!'

Madeleine smiled, pleased for Sandie, but she was thoughtful for a few moments before she said, 'Sandie, you won't get too—too keen, will you dear?'

'Too keen?' Sandie looked at her, her cheeks colouring. 'It's only a dinner date.'

Madeleine looked uncomfortable. 'I know, but he *is* very attractive and at your age it's easy to get hurt.' Sandie opened her mouth to protest but her stepmother put out a hand to stop her. 'No, listen to me. He's quite a lot older than you and his life-style, his status—even if . . .'

Sandie laughed and gave her a hug. 'Oh, Maddie! I'm quite able to handle the situation. I'm not a starry-eyed teenager any more, you know. I'm quite capable of controlling my emotions. I agree that Drew is attractive, but I'm quite sure that there isn't the slightest chance of anything developing between us!'

Madeleine looked at her for a long moment, a wistful sadness in her eyes. 'Oh, Sandie,' she said at last. 'I can remember saying the very same words to myself on the night I first went out with your father! And before I knew what was happening to me I was head over heels in love with him. So much so, that I didn't know whether I was coming or going! It can be very painful—so be warned, love.'

Later, when she was alone, Sandie thought about what Madeleine had said. She wondered just how old Drew really was. Surely the age-gap couldn't be as great as all that? She wondered why he had never married and how experienced he was with women. Closing her eyes she tried to remember his kiss, but it was impossible—like trying to remember a half-forgotten dream.

CHAPTER FOUR

THE FOLLOWING evening Sandie tried on at least four different dresses and took them all off again. She stood in her room, an assortment of clothes laid out on her bed, biting her lip in an agony of indecision. For one thing she hadn't a clue where Drew might be taking her, and for another she didn't have any idea what kind of feminine attire appealed to him. So far he had seen her either in jeans or in her uniform. But he must be used to sophisticated women, she reasoned, having a sister who was a model. And what would they talk about? She imagined the sparklingly witty conversation he must be accustomed to with his elegant friends. Would she dry up the minute she was with him, unable to think of a thing to say, just as she had yesterday? In a panic she toyed with the idea of ringing him to say she had a cold, a headache—*the plague!*

At last she chose a simple black velvet skirt and a filmy top in a delicate shade of silvery green that looked well with her tawny hair. The silky material clung to her slim figure and enhanced the creaminess of her complexion. She made up her face carefully and piled her hair up into a top-knot, leaving tendrils escaping at the hairline to soften the severity of the style. At last she was ready and glanced at the clock as she sprayed on a touch of perfume. Eight o'clock he had said. It was five minutes to. Did she go down and wait for him in the hall or should she stay where she was until he arrived, and then make him wait for her?

She didn't have to decide. At exactly eight she heard his car pull up on the drive downstairs. A moment later the front doorbell rang and she heard the murmur of voices as Mrs Simmons, the house-keeper, let him in. Madeleine had decided to avoid him and had taken the car and driven into Hartmoor to the cinema.

Sandie opened the door of her room and made her way across the landing on wobbly legs. Drew was waiting at the foot of the stairs, his back towards her, and she took a deep breath as she started down, fixing her eyes on the glossy blue-black head with its fascinating silver streak. She had almost reached the bottom when he turned suddenly and looked up.

'Good evening, Sandie. How delightful you look.'

'Good evening—oh!' Whether it was because she had lost her point of focus when he turned his head, or whether she caught her heel in the carpet, she never knew, but the next moment she stumbled awkwardly. He stepped forward and caught her by the shoulders as she clutched desperately at the banister rail.

'There, steady. Are you all right?'

Her heart sank with dismay as she looked up at him. She could have burst into tears. Why was it that each time they met something embarrassing happened? Tonight she had tried so hard to be elegant and sophisticated. Suddenly she was very aware of the warmth of his hands on her shoulders and his breath on her cheek. The dark grey eyes held that now familiar flicker of amusement as they looked down at her, though his voice was concerned as he asked,

'Did you hurt your ankle? That was quite a twist you gave it. Would you like me to look at it?'

'No, honestly. It's fine, thank you.' Her voice was just a shade too bright and she knew her cheeks were scarlet. He must think her absolutely hopeless! They went out to the car in silence and she allowed him to help her into the passenger seat. When they were on the road he glanced at her.

'I thought we might go to a little club I know. it's quiet and the food is excellent. I think you'll like it.'

For a moment Sandie was silent. Then she said miserably, 'I can't think why you asked me out. You must think me the clumsiest, most stupid girl you've ever met. I think you're right to choose a quiet place. You wouldn't want any of your friends to see you dining with an idiot like me, would you?'

The moment the words were out she bit her lips hard. What on earth had made her say a thing like that? If only she could learn to keep her mouth shut!

To her surprise, Drew braked and drew the car into the side of the road. Switching off the engine he turned to look at her, his eyes serious.

'Tell me quite truthfully, Sandie. Do I really make you feel like that? Do I give the impression of being so stuffy?'

'No! No, of course not!' She gazed at him imploringly, her green eyes brimming with tears. 'It's just that something always *happens* when I meet you— things that never happen with anyone else.' She sniffed hard and he handed her a large white handkerchief.

'Maybe it would help if we talked about it,' he suggested quietly.

She dabbed at her eyes with the handkerchief, hoping it wasn't making her mascara run. 'Yes, I think it would. I'm not accident-prone at all, really,' she assured him. 'Usually I'm a calm, sane person. Well, how else could I be a nurse? And— and you said that there is no such thing as an accident, so how do you explain the way I spill things on you, fall on you and bump into you every time we meet? It's not—' She trailed off as she heard him beginning to laugh. Not the deep-throated laugh she had heard before, but a gentle chuckle. He reached out to cup her chin with one hand, bringing her face round to look at him. His eyes danced with merriment as they smiled down into hers.

'I wonder if you have any idea of how flattering all this is, Sandie,' he said. 'I had no idea at all that I was capable of producing that kind of effect in a woman.'

She winced painfully. Somehow she'd managed to do it *again*, and now he was openly laughing at her naivety. Swiftly he bent and kissed her on the mouth.

'Forgive me,' he whispered. 'I really didn't mean to tease you, and I meant what I said. I haven't felt so flattered or so light-hearted for a long time.' He smiled at her, his face very close to hers. 'Don't change, Sandie. You're perfect just the way you are, accidents and all. And as for not wanting to be seen dining with you, I know I shall be the envy of every other man in the room! Now, shall we go?'

She nodded, feeling rather numb. 'Well, yes please, I'd like to—if you're sure.'

'I am.' He straightened in his seat and switched on the ignition again, his eyes on the road. Sandie pinched herself surreptitiously. Yes, it really was happening. Maybe, if she kept her fingers firmly crossed, this evening wouldn't turn out to be another disaster after all!

The club was quiet and intimate and Sandie would have enjoyed the meal very much but for one thing. As she ate the delicious things that Drew ordered for her, she became increasingly aware of her twisted ankle. When they had settled themselves at the table she had slipped her foot out of her shoe but now, as she tried to put it on again, she could hardly squeeze it back. Drew noticed the stricken look on her face.

'Is anything wrong?'

'It's my ankle, I'm afraid,' she told him. 'I must have twisted it more than I thought. It seems to be quite swollen.'

He stood up and took her arm. 'Do you think you can manage as far as the car park?'

She nodded, gritting her teeth determinedly. 'I'm sure I can.'

As he opened the car door for her five minutes later, she sank gratefully into the passenger seat. He bent and examined the injured ankle, probing it with gentle fingers.

'Mmm, just a sprain, I'd say. It's a good thing you're going to be off for a few days. It'll need rest. What it needs at the moment is a cold compress to reduce the swelling.' He went round to his own side of the car and got in, glancing at her. 'Look, I have a flat in Hartmoor, quite close to the hospital. I use it when I want to stay close at hand. If we went there now I could see to that for you. It really should be attended to as soon as possible.' He smiled. 'I make rather good coffee, too. What do you say?'

'I could easily put a compress on it myself when I get home. I don't want to be any trouble,' she told him.

'Ah, but *will* you?' He shook his head at her. 'I'd like to make sure it was all right. After all, it was because of me, wasn't it?'

The flat was in a smart private block on the outskirts of town and they went up in the lift to the fourth floor. It was a small, modest flat with none of the grandness of Snow House. Sandie felt more at home there. Somehow it seemed to make their relationship more relaxed. In the tiny kitchen Drew ran cold water into a bowl and added ice cubes from the refrigerator, then took a clean cloth from a drawer. Sandie took them firmly from him.

'I'll do it while you make that famous coffee you were telling me about.'

'Are you sure you can manage?'

She laughed. 'I wouldn't be much of a nurse if I couldn't, now would I?'

He went with her into the living-room and pulled up a stool for her to rest the injured foot.

'It might be as well if you were to pop into X-ray in the morning, just to make sure, but I'd advise you to rest it for a couple of days.'

She sighed. 'I was looking forward to riding again during my break. I enjoyed myself so much that

Sunday at Snow House that I'd thought of looking up the local stables and taking it up regularly again,' she told him. 'But now—'

'Don't look so disappointed. Twenty-four hours can make all the difference if it's only a sprain. After that, if you want a gentle ride, you can take Sheila out. The exercise will do her good. She's beginning to get rather tubby.' He smiled. 'The lad who looks after the stables for me is called Joe Spence. He's a good lad. Tell him I said it was all right for you to take her.'

She stared at him, her cheeks going pink. 'Oh, that would be lovely. Are you really sure you can trust me with her?'

'I don't make offers I'm not sure about,' he said abruptly. 'I'll get back to the coffee then, while you attend to that ankle.'

She stared at his retreating back as he left the room. *Now* what had she said?

He returned after a short time with the tray, to find the swollen ankle responding well to the cold compress. He smiled at her as he put the tray down on a low table.

'That looks better already.'

She looked up at him apologetically. 'I feel such a fool.'

'Why?'

'Well, it's hardly the ideal way to end a romant— a glamorous evening.' She felt her cheeks blazing and hurried on in a panicky attempt to cover the embarrassing slip. 'I'm sure you don't usually end your dinner dates by bringing the lady back to your flat and putting her on the settee. Oh!' Why couldn't she learn to keep her mouth shut?

As Drew bent over the coffee cups it was clear that he was having a hard time keeping a straight face. He handed her a cup of steaming, fragrant coffee, his lips twitching.

'Drink this and tell me what you think of my one culinary talent.' He sat down beside her with his own cup. 'As a matter of interest, you're the first lady to see the inside of this flat—apart from my sister, of course. She helped me furnish it.' His eyes twinkled at her. 'Furthermore, you're the first to test the comfort of the settee.' He stood up and went over to the music centre that took up almost the whole of one side of the room. 'What kind of music do you like?' He turned to look at her speculatively. 'A little Chopin or Rachmaninov— or are you into heavy rock, as they say?'

He was making fun of her again, but she had to admit that she deserved it. 'Rachmaninov would be lovely,' she said. 'Do you have his second piano concerto?'

'I do indeed.' He slipped in a cassette and switched on and a moment later the opening notes of the first movement filled the room. Drew returned to her side, glancing at her as he sat down.

'You have very romantic taste in music.'

She looked at him with a wry smile. 'I suppose you'd expect me to choose clog-dancing music, or perhaps a little tune on the alpenhorn!'

He laughed, his eyes crinkling at the corners and the strong line of his mouth softening. She relaxed and laughed with him.

'You were right about the coffee,' she said, taking a sip. 'It really is good.' She looked at him over the rim of the cup. 'You obviously like music. Do you play yourself?'

His eyebrows rose a fraction. 'It's odd you should ask. Yes, I do. As a matter of fact, there was a time when I thought I might make it my career; I even spent a year at music college.'

She looked at him with interest. 'Oh, you haven't always wanted to be a doctor then?'

He shook his head. 'I came from a family of medical men. When it was time for me to choose a career I felt there was too much pressure on me to follow suit. I'd always liked music and I thought I had talent, so I tried it.'

'But you changed your mind?'

'Yes. I suppose I'd always known what I wanted really, but that year helped me to make up my own mind and that was important to me.'

'But you still play, and enjoy it?' she asked, her head on one side.

'Oh yes, for my own amusement.' He listened to the music for a moment, his eyes softening with appreciation as the swelling theme filled the room. 'I have to admit that when I listen to pianists like this I feel a little sad that I haven't more talent.'

'I'd like to hear you play someday,' Sandie said shyly.

He looked at her. 'Tell me more about that stepmother of yours,' he said suddenly. 'I'm intrigued to know why she was so interested in my sister yesterday. And, incidentally, how she knew about her visits to Snow House. Anita hasn't been down since you moved into Elm Court.'

Sandie looked into her cup, squirming inwardly. 'I'm afraid it was me,' she admitted. 'But I wasn't gossiping. I saw the name-tape in the hat you lent me. Madeleine asked me what I'd done for a riding hat and I told her you'd lent me one that belonged to someone called Anita Banks. It might sound awful, but I hadn't heard of her.'

'But your stepmother had?'

She nodded. 'Yes. Well, she's always reading the fashion magazines and going to see the latest designer collections, that sort of thing.' Mentally she crossed her fingers. She hadn't exactly fibbed, just sort of re-moulded the truth. She couldn't afford to damage her image any further.

'And she'd be intrigued to meet a well-known model,' Drew supplied.

Sandie shook her head. 'It isn't only that. She's finding it rather hard, adjusting to being alone. She'd like to get to know people and make some lasting friendships.'

He looked at her thoughtfully for a moment. 'You care a great deal about her, don't you?'

She sighed. 'Of course. We're very close. Sometimes I feel that Dad was misguided in marrying her.'

He frowned. 'In what way?'

'Well, I wonder sometimes if he thought he should marry to provide me with a mother. After all, Maddie was much nearer to my age than his.'

Drew's eyebrows arched. 'Well, I suppose that would be a logical conclusion for a young girl to come to.' He reached out to cup her chin with his hand. 'But it does rather give away the fact that you don't know very much about men.' His eyes drew hers for a moment and she felt mesmerised by them. In their dark grey depths she could see—

what? Laughter, tolerance, curiosity? Feeling awkward she pulled her head back slightly, disengaging her chin from his fingers.

'I—I'd better be going,' she muttered, bending to find her shoe. 'It must be getting late.'

'Don't put too much weight on that ankle,' he warned, getting up with her.

She pushed her foot into the shoe and took a step forward, but although her foot felt so much better, she found that the ankle was still weak. It gave under her and she stumbled.

'Oh!'

He caught her by the elbows. 'There, what did I tell you?' He stepped closer, encircling her waist with one arm while the other hand tilted her face up towards his.

'Does it hurt?' His eyes searched hers.

She shook her head. 'No,' she said breathlessly. 'It's just—' Again his eyes held hers, almost hypnotically. Then his face came nearer and she closed her eyes as his mouth covered hers. His kiss was hard, just as it had been that Sunday two weeks ago. It was almost as though he was putting his stamp on her—claiming her. The thought spun dizzily in Sandie's brain as his lips crushed hers a second time, defying response. Then suddenly their pressure eased and he raised his head to look down at her.

'You can't go yet,' he said quietly. 'Don't you want to hear the rest of the music?'

Looking into his eyes, Sandie felt that he was speaking of more than just the concerto and she was suddenly afraid. Her own violent response to the pressure of his body startled her. It had taken her unawares, engulfing her like a tidal wave. Did he know? Could he sense the desire that blazed up in her like a flame? But before she could do anything about it he was kissing her again, his lips tender on hers now, teasing them persuasively till the fear and tension melted and she relaxed, reassured, in his arms. Slowly they sank back on to the settee and he drew her head on to his shoulder with a sigh.

'If this was a film or a play I'd probably be telling you I hadn't meant this to happen,' he told her. 'But I can tell you now that I've wanted it to happen ever since the day you almost hurled yourself at me.'

He turned her face towards him and kissed her again. This time she allowed her lips to part softly beneath his, her heart pounding as the kiss deepened and became intimate—exploring, setting her senses aflame again. In the background, almost as though it were playing inside her own head, the music swelled. The great love theme of the concerto seemed to uncoil her inhibitions and she found herself responding to him eagerly, her arms creeping inside his jacket to feel the warmth of his skin and the strong, vibrant beat of his heart that matched her own. His mouth left hers and traced a line of kisses from her ear to the base of her throat, where the fluttering pulse betrayed her excitement. His lips paused, warm and sensuous.

'I wonder if you have the slightest idea what you do to me, Sandie,' he whispered.

'Tell me.'

He laughed softly. 'You were the first person, the first woman, to make me laugh for a long time.'

'Oh—all those terrible blunders?' she asked disappointedly.

He shook his head. 'Don't be ashamed of them. You're so refreshingly different, so unsophisticated and sweet. Being with you is like—like a walk in the woods after a storm.' He looked at her crestfallen face and laughed softly, nuzzling her neck. 'I think we were meant to meet. I told you once that there is a theory that there's no such thing as an accident; my grandmother believed that. Every time something unpleasant happened to any of us she'd say that there was a reason for it and that one day that reason would be made clear. She believed that we make our own destiny.'

Sandie twisted her head to look up at him. 'Are you saying that I made those awful things happen on purpose?'

He smiled. 'Perhaps, subconsciously. Why, aren't you pleased with the outcome?'

She didn't reply but pressed her head into the hollow of his shoulder. 'Do you really believe in all that?' she asked.

He shrugged. 'I haven't worked with the brain all this time without knowing that the human mind is a very complex piece of machinery.'

'And do you think I'll go on having accidents every time we meet?' Now it was her turn to tease. Her green eyes sparkled as she lifted her head to look up at him and his arms tightened around her.

'You're very lovely when you look at me like that, but you'd be even lovelier with your hair down.' He began to take the pins out of her hair while she protested, laughing and trying to catch at his hands. But at last the thick skein dropped on to her neck and uncoiled itself brightly about her shoulders. He ran his fingers through it admiringly, burying his face in the tawny mass. 'Mmm, you smell like a flower after an April shower.' His hands framed her face, twisting themselves into her hair so that she could not escape. His eyes burned into hers as he drew her towards him.

'Darling Sandie, do you know how beautiful you are?' His lips claimed hers again, this time possessively, parting them once more to tease and explore till she could hear the blood singing in her ears. She felt his fingers unfastening the buttons of the filmy evening top and gasped as they made contact with her bare skin, making her spine tingle. Without taking his mouth from hers he slid the soft material from her shoulder and ran his hand caressingly over the rising swell of one small breast.

'Sandie—' His lips moved against hers as his fingers explored further, sliding round to trace the line of her spine and pull her hard against him, 'Sandie, Sandie—'

All her resolve, all her resistance, flew away like ash on the wind and she clung to him, tugging at the buttons of his shirt until she too made contact with the warm skin beneath. She heard him catch his breath as she pressed her fingers convulsively into the flesh of his back, arching her own, her head falling back, lips parted, eyes closed in ecstasy as she felt the warmth of his skin against hers. She heard her own voice murmuring incoherent words of love as she wound her arms about his neck and felt the weight of his body press down on hers . . . Then suddenly he was disentangling her. Holding her two hands in his he looked down at her gravely.

'I'll take you home, Sandie. You were right, it is getting late.'

Her eyes flew open disbelievingly and she stared at him. How could he switch off so abruptly? Inside her the excitement hung suspended, leaving her feeling weak and shaky.

'What is it? What have I done?' Her eyes filled with tears. But he was fastening the buttons of her top, tidying her as though she were a child. His eyes met hers and he bent to kiss her lightly.

'You've done nothing, darling, except almost make me lose control,' he told her, his voice hoarse. 'Now, where did I put your coat?' He stood up, looking round the room as he straightened his tie and smoothed the rumpled shirt. He glanced at his watch. 'If I hurry, I can still get you home before midnight.'

Suddenly angry she sprang up from the settee, mindless of her swollen ankle. 'I don't turn into a pumpkin if that's what's troubling you!' she shouted. 'I'm not a child! How—how dare you treat me like one?' She was dangerously close to tears— tears of frustration and humiliation—and she fought hard for control, swallowing at the knot in her throat, clenching and unclenching her hands.

He picked up her coat and crossed the room to her, slipping it round her shoulders and allowing his arms to remain there as he looked down into her eyes.

'Sandie, darling, don't be hurt. You're very young—' He pressed a finger against her lips as she opened them to protest. 'Yes you are, to me, anyway. A great deal younger than me, at any rate. I have no intention of taking advantage of that.'

'Why not?' she asked plaintively.

A flicker of wistful amusement lit his eyes for a second before he replied, 'Because you deserve better. You're sweet and wholesome and extremely desirable and it would be all too easy for me to seduce you here and now.' He smiled wryly. 'In fact the thought of it is making me weak at the knees at this very moment.' His hands on her shoulders tightened as he looked deep into her eyes. 'But I'm not going to, Sandie. Unless I'm very much mistaken, I'd be your first lover.'

She bit her lip. 'I can't think of anyone I'd rather—' Again he stopped her, a finger against her lips.

'You may think that at this moment, but somewhere out there there's a boy of your own age waiting for you. Someone who likes discos and pop concerts, motor bikes—all the things that young people ought to enjoy.'

She shook her head. 'But I hate all those things. It doesn't follow! Oh, please, Drew, don't send me away like this!' She reached up, clasping her hands at the back of his head and drawing it down to hers. Her lips found his. For a moment he resisted, but their soft persistence was irresistible. In a breathtaking movement he caught her to him and she felt the quickened beat of his heart as he crushed her close, but a second later he had released her and taken a step backwards. He pulled her coat round her, buttoning it to the neck and fixing her with a resolute look.

'Downstairs, young lady, and into that car this minute!'

On the drive back to Elm Court they were silent,

each occupied with their own thoughts. Sandie knew without a shadow of doubt that she was in love with him—helplessly, hopelessly, totally in love—and she could think of nothing that was likely to change that. He, on the other hand, obviously was not. Attracted, yes. Enough to want to make love to her, but nothing more.

She glanced sideways at the strong profile. Concentration had set his features into hard lines and it was difficult now to imagine the intense, smouldering look in his eyes when he had kissed her. She thought of his words—*You're young—a great deal younger than me*. Was that the only reason, she wondered. As the car came to a halt at the gates of Elm Court she turned to look at him.

'Drew, can I ask you something? Is it—is it just because of the difference in our ages? Because if it is, you don't have to worry. I told you, my parents were older than most people's Everyone says I'm mature for my years and, anyway, I don't care two hoots about any of the things you mentioned.'

He looked into the large, luminous eyes for a moment, then reached out to draw her close, pressing her head against his shoulder and stroking her hair.

'Oh, Sandie, what am I going to do about you?' he whispered.

She looked up at him. 'You won't turn your back on me, will you? You won't try to ignore me, pretend I don't exist? I don't think I could bear that.'

He sighed deeply. 'Oh God! What have I started?' he murmured, half under his breath. He kissed her forehead. 'I think you know that it would be far better if I did—better and kinder and far more sensible in the long run.' He looked down into her eyes, dark with hurt. 'But it probably doesn't surprise you to know that kind and sensible are the last things I feel at this moment!' Very gently he pushed her away. 'And now say good-night like the nice, polite child you are, before I forget my age again!'

The twinkle was back in his eyes as he said it and she relaxed a little. So he didn't intend to end their relationship completely—there *was* still a chance. She reached up to kiss him briefly, then opened the door and got quickly out of the car before he could change his mind.

CHAPTER FIVE

SANDIE spent the following day on the settee in the drawing-room at Elm Court with her feet up. Her ankle had been almost back to normal when she got up, but Madeleine had insisted.

'If Drew said you should rest it then you must,' she said. 'After all, he should know. You are sure it isn't broken or anything, aren't you?'

Sandie shook her head. 'It's only a bad sprain. He did say that if it was any worse this morning I should look in at X-ray, but the swelling's almost gone now, so there's no need.'

It was a beautiful day and she lay in front of the open French windows, enjoying a view of the garden and dreaming of the previous evening and all that had happened. She racked her brain to think of a way she could convince Drew that she was mature enough for him. It was strange. From what he had said, it was her youth that had attracted him, yet, for the very same reason, he was trying to reject her. She closed her eyes, enjoying the caress of the sun on their lids, reliving Drew's kisses and the touch of his hands, her heart contracting with longing. Somehow she *would* find a way to make him fall in love with her—want her so much that he couldn't let her go. The thought filled her entire being. Nothing seemed more important at that moment.

By the next day the ankle was completely recovered and Sandie was bored with inactivity. The weather was holding and in the morning she took Maddie's car and drove into Hartmoor to buy herself a riding hat and a pair of boots. Over lunch she told Madeleine that Drew had offered her the use of his horses in his absence. Her stepmother looked pleased.

'You haven't said much about your evening with him. I take it you had a good time?'

Sandie nodded. 'Very nice, thank you.'

Madeleine looked closely at her. 'Is that all I'm going to hear? Sandie, you weren't offended by what I said to you the other day, were you? I don't mean to interfere, you know.'

Sandie looked up with a smile. 'Of course I wasn't offended.' She hesitated, hoping that Madeleine wouldn't probe any further, but at that moment Mrs Simmons came in to clear the table and she was able to change the subject without it looking obvious.

After lunch she changed into the new hat and boots and set out for Snow House in pleasant anticipation of an afternoon's riding. As she cycled along the lane, she tried to remember the name of the stable boy—Joe something. Smith? No, Spence. Yes, that was it.

She found him in the stables, spreading clean straw in the empty loose boxes and started to explain why she was here.

'Mr Maxwell said that I could ride Sheila. I'm a nurse at the same hospital and I live here in the village too,' she added as the boy stared at her. By the doubtful look on his face she would need all the qualifications she could think of!

He was a short, stocky lad with a thatch of sandy

hair which he ran a hand through as he looked at her.

'I can ride,' she assured him. 'And I have been here before. I'll take good care of her, you needn't worry.'

'It ain't that, miss,' the boy told her. 'It's just that Sheila belongs to Miss Anita.'

'Yes, I know that.' Sandie was beginning to wonder if the boy thought her half-witted when another voice behind them spoke up.

'Perhaps I can clear up the misunderstanding.'

Sandie turned to see a tall, dark-haired girl standing smiling at her from the doorway. Immediately she knew that this was Drew's sister. She had the same wide-set eyes and glossy dark hair, the same ease of movement and air of quiet assurance. She wore jeans and a yellow sweater.

'Drew didn't know I'd be home when he made you the offer,' she said. 'Unfortunately I was riding Sheila this morning when she cast a shoe, so I rode her over to Leech End to the farrier.'

'I see—well that's all right. I'll go,' Sandie said.

'Oh, please don't do that! I'm sorry you've come for nothing. Won't you come inside and have some tea with me?' the girl offered. 'I was really bored by myself. I'd appreciate the company.' She held out her hand. 'I'm Anita Banks, by the way.'

Sandie smiled. 'And I'm Sandie Masters. I'm a staff nurse at Hartmoor General. I live with my stepmother just down the road at Elm Court.'

Anita opened a side door and held it for Sandie to pass through in front of her. 'Your stepmother— ah, yes. She would be the one who kindly invited us to a dinner party.'

'That's right—so Drew told you?'

They went into a small, cosy room overlooking the stable yard. Anita called unceremoniously through the open door, 'Make us a pot of tea, will you, Libby? We're in the morning room.' As she closed the door she smiled at Sandie. 'Tell me, have you known Drew long?' she asked.

Sandie was a little taken aback at her directness. 'Oh no, not all that long. I've only been at Hartmoor for about a month.'

'And that's where you met?'

'Yes. We didn't get off to a very good start,' Sandie told her. 'Every time I came into contact with him something terrible seemed to happen. But I believe things are improving now.'

Anita looked hard at her. 'I think the mist is beginning to clear! He didn't have a date with you the night before last, did he?'

Sandie blushed. 'Well, yes, as a matter of fact he did. We went out to dinner, but even then I had to upset things by twisting my ankle. He had to take me to the Hartmoor flat and put a cold compress on it.'

Anita looked amused. 'Well! What an interesting variation on the "etchings" theme!' At that moment the door opened and a fair-haired young woman came in with the tray of tea. As the door closed behind her Anita started to pour, looking thoughtfully at Sandie.

'So you hit it off pretty well with Drew, in spite of the shaky start?'

Sandie met the cool, perceptive eyes. 'I think so, yes.' She sipped her tea, avoiding the other girl's steady gaze.

'Well,' Anita took a biscuit from the plate on the

tray and bit into it, 'I knew as soon as I arrived that something special had happened to him. He's been mooning around like a love-sick schoolboy. I can hardly get a word out of him!'

'Oh? I expect he must be concerned about a patient—it can't possibly have anything to do with me.' Sandie searched her mind frantically for a change of subject. 'When Drew let me ride your mare he also lent me your hat and boots,' she said. Anita smiled.

'Good. It's a pity we couldn't ride again today.'

'I wondered who Anita Banks could be,' Sandie confessed. 'I'm sorry to say I didn't know your name. It was Maddie, my stepmother, who told me you were a model.'

Anita laughed. 'You must have thought that Drew had a secret love! The reason we have different names, by the way, is that I was married once.' She sighed. 'Unhappily it didn't work out. It seems that unsuccessful relationships with the opposite sex are something that runs in our family!' She replaced her cup on the tray and walked over to the window to look out. Sandie wanted to encourage her to expand on her last remark, but before she could think of a way of doing so the other girl turned to her with a smile.

'It's such a lovely afternoon. It seems a sin to be cooped up indoors. Would you like to come for a walk?'

For a while they walked in silence but all the time Sandie was aware of Anita's cool appraisal.

'Do you like living here?' she asked at last.

Sandie nodded. 'It's lovely, though I live at the nurses' home at Hartmoor for most of the time. I only come home when I'm off duty. Since my father died my stepmother is trying to make a new life for herself and I think she'll do that better on her own.'

Anita raised her eyebrows. 'Haven't you thought of cutting loose?'

Sandie shrugged. 'It's always easier said than done, isn't it? Besides, I feel sort of responsible for her.' She glanced at Anita. 'I didn't mean that quite the way it sounded. She's a very independent person. It's just that she's missing my father badly. She's always been a good stepmother to me and I see this as a way of repaying her.'

Anita smiled. 'It sounds as though you have a very nice relationship with her. I almost envy you. I lost my own mother when I was quite young but I wasn't as lucky as you.'

They continued in silence for a while and Sandie reflected that she had told this girl more about herself in the past hour than she usuallly disclosed in a month. It must be something to do with her relaxed, friendly manner.

They reached the ridge that overlooked the valley and Anita stood still, drawing in a deep breath.

'Mmm—smell that air. Isn't it fantastic? Thank God I have this place to come home to! You know, when I was a little girl, Snow House was always full of people and laughter. Our mother loved company. But when she and Father parted all that ended.' She sighed. 'Ah well. If Drew ever marries, Snow House will have a mistress again and maybe those days will come back. I'd like that.'

For a moment as she looked out across the valley her lovely face was sad. Then she turned to Sandie with a smile.

'I'm really glad to have met you this afternoon, Sandie. I hope we'll be friends. Shall we walk back now?'

Sandie returned to Hartmoor the following morning feeling refreshed. She had thoroughly enjoyed her break and looked forward to her work with renewed energy. During her break nothing dramatic had happened on the ward, but that morning, just before lunch, the telephone rang in Sister's office. The call was from Casualty. A new patient was on the way up—a road traffic accident victim, a young girl with a severe head injury. Sandie took notes. A blood sample had been taken for cross-matching and blood was on its way; meanwhile the child was already on a saline drip. She was deeply unconscious and had breathing difficulties. Mr Maxwell had been bleeped but he was in theatre. The Casualty Officer had performed an emergency tracheotomy.

Sandie replaced the receiver and hurried out into the ward to find Sister, who was accompanying Mr Crabtree on his round. In minutes the patient arrived, wheeled carefully by two porters while a nurse held the saline bottle aloft. For the following few minutes everyone was galvanised into action as the patient was transferred into bed. A technician arrived from the Path Lab with the new supply of blood and the drip was set up. Sandie looked down at the small figure in the bed, her head swathed in bandages. She couldn't be more than ten or eleven and she looked in a very bad way, her little face swollen and discoloured with bruising.

'Do you have any details about her?' she asked

the nurse from Casualty. 'Was she with her parents?'

The girl shook her head. 'It seems she was riding a bicycle and collided with a lorry. The driver is still down in Casualty, being treated for shock. He was giving a statement to the police the last time I saw him.'

'Did she have any identification?' Sandie asked. 'Have you been able to contact anyone about her?'

'Yes. Luckily she was wearing one of those pendant things. It's been handed to the police. All I know is her name—Donna Fenning.'

Drew arrived at that moment and the rest of the nurses dispersed as he made his examination, firing staccato questions at Sister as he did so. His face was grave as he bent over the child.

'I'll arrange to have her X-rayed up here,' he said at last, straightening up. 'Though I doubt if there's a great deal we can do at this stage. There's obviously a massive oedema.' He looked at Sister. 'Let's get that blood into her and keep her monitored until the swelling goes down. Do we know who she is?'

'She was wearing an identity pendant,' Sister replied. 'Her name is Donna Fenning. I understand the next of kin are being informed.'

He nodded. 'Good. I'd like to get her on to a ventilator as soon as possible. In the meantime take the routine fifteen minute checks and regular blood samples to test for blood gasses. If there's any change let me know at once.'

Sister walked with him to the ward entrance. 'Do you want to see the parents when they arrive?'

'I'll be available if they ask, of course, though

there's very little I can tell them at this stage.'

When he had gone, Sister Milton looked at Sandie. 'I'd like you to take charge of her, Staff. She'll need to be very closely monitored. I think you'd better sit with her for the first few hours at least.' She glanced at her watch. 'I forgot! You haven't had your lunch-break yet, have you? You'd better go now. I'll stay with her till you get back.'

In the canteen Sandie found she had little appetite. She couldn't get the small bruised face out of her mind. That kind of accident was so frightening. One minute that child had been cycling along without a care in the world, and the next, she was lying under the wheels of a lorry. Human life was so frail—so easily snuffed out. Sandie's heart went out to the child's parents waiting at home. It had hurt to lose her father, but the death of a child was even more traumatic. She took a deep breath. Donna wasn't going to die though—not if it was humanly possible to save her. Hurriedly she forced down the rest of her meal and drank her coffee. The best thing she could do was to get back to the ward as soon as she could.

She heard the commotion as soon as she got out of the lift. A woman's voice was raised hysterically. Sister Milton's voice could be heard too, remonstrating in a sort of stage whisper.

'*Please!*—I must ask you to keep your voice down. I have five very sick patients in the ward. I really cannot have them disturbed like this. I've told you, I've already sent for Mr Maxwell. He'll be here as soon as he can, I'm sure.'

As Sandie turned in through the glass doors she saw the back of the hysterical woman. She wore a beautiful pastel mink coat and her gleaming blonde hair was elaborately dressed. There was something vaguely familiar about her and when she turned her face, Sandie recognised her at once as Eve Paul, the singer she had seen so many times on TV. As soon as the woman noticed Sandie she stepped forward and seized her by the arm.

'Perhaps I can get some sense out of you! Will you tell someone to get that horrible thing out of Donna's throat. She'll be scarred for life! Who did it to her anyway? And who gave them permission? When I find that person I'll have them thrown out of here!'

Sister threw Sandie an appealing look and walked into her office. Sandie moved towards the ward entrance, drawing the woman with her. 'I take it that you are Donna's mother? Shall we just talk outside?'

The woman gave a derisive snort. 'If we must, though I'd like to protest strongly about the way I've been treated. That ignorant woman,' she glared towards Sister's office, 'didn't even recognise me!'

'I do,' Sandie said tactfully. 'You're Eve Paul, aren't you?'

The woman looked slightly appeased. 'Thank God! Sanity at last,' she breathed.

'Perhaps you'd like me to get you a cup of tea while you're waiting. There's a small waiting-room just along the corridor. You'll be more comfortable in there.' Sandie began to walk towards it but Eve wasn't to be so easily persuaded.

'No, I insist on seeing the doctor in charge at once!' she demanded, shaking Sandie's hand from her arm. 'And I'm staying with Donna until I do.'

'Your daughter is unconscious. There isn't really anything you can do,' Sandie told her. 'Believe me, I know how helpless you must feel, but everything possible is being done for her. She really is in good hands.'

Eve stared at her. 'How can you expect me to believe that?' she asked hysterically. 'No one is doing a thing! She's just lying there with that awful tube stuck in her throat.'

'When Donna was admitted she had breathing difficulties. The tube in her throat is to help her to breathe,' Sandie told her patiently, wondering vaguely who had allowed her into Intensive Care without preparing her. 'At present Donna has a lot of swelling. Until it goes down a little the doctors can't see just what damage has been done. I'm sure that Mr Maxwell will explain everything to you as soon as he—' She broke off as the lift doors opened and Drew stepped out. 'Ah, here he is now,' she said with a sigh of relief.

Eve turned, opening her mouth to repeat her tirade into a fresh pair of ears, then stopped as she came face to face with Drew.

'My God, it can't be!' she exclaimed, her mouth dropping open in amazement. Then she burst into tears and threw herself into his arms. 'Drew! Oh, darling, please help my baby. No one here understands how I feel—they're all *idiots!*'

Drew's startled eyes met Sandie's over Eve's bowed head. Quietly she withdrew and tapped on Sister's door. 'Mr Maxwell is here,' she told her. 'How is Donna?'

Sister glanced at her watch. 'Due for another

blood sample. I left Nurse Freeman in charge while I dealt with that woman. She burst in here like a hurricane and demanded all sorts of outrageous things. Where is she now?' She peered round in a way that, in ordinary circumstances, Sandie would have found comic.

'In the corridor with Mr Maxwell,' she told her. 'It seems they know one another. By the way, didn't you recognise her? She's Eve Paul, the singer.'

Sister Milton sniffed disapprovingly. 'As far as *I'm* concerned, she's the child's mother. There are no celebrities on *my* ward!'

Sandie took over from Nurse Freeman, taking the routine blood sample, doing the observations and entering the results on the chart at the end of the bed. She had just finished when Drew came in with Eve, Sister bringing up the rear, her face still quite clearly disapproving. Drew looked at the chart and made a brief examination. He looked at Sandie.

'I've just explained to Sister that Miss Paul is Donna's stepmother, her next of kin. I've given her permission to visit at any time, though I have explained that Donna may be unconscious for some time.'

Eve looked up at him with brimming eyes. Her abusive, demanding manner had changed now for one of pleading submissiveness. 'I want her moved to the private wing, Drew,' she whined. 'I don't like this place. Please, can't you arrange it for me?'

Drew looked at Sister, who stared back at him in horror. 'Donna can't be moved at present,' he told Eve. 'This is the Intensive Care Unit and all the special equipment she needs is here. But the moment she can be moved I will let you know and we'll see what can be arranged.'

'And if an operation is necessary it will be you who does it, won't it, darling? I wouldn't let anyone else touch her.'

Drew looked uncomfortable. 'I can assure you that all the surgeons in this hospital are equally skilled,' he told her. 'Though it is quite likely that I shall be operating. We shall have to see.' He took Eve by the arm and began to move away. 'And now I think you should let Donna get some rest. There really isn't anything you can do to help her at the moment.'

When they had disappeared through the ward doors Sister snorted. 'What an awful woman! I can't say I'm looking forward to her being under my feet day and night!'

'I have a feeling that Mr Maxwell knew what he was doing when he gave her permission to visit at any time,' Sandie said. 'If she had been denied it she might well have made a fuss. As it is, she'll probably calm down now.'

Sister pursed her lips. 'I must say he seemed to know how to handle her. I wonder how they came to meet. She doesn't seem his type at all.'

Sandie wondered too, though she didn't say so. When it was time to go off duty she was reluctant to leave the ward. There was still no change in Donna Fenning's condition, which in many ways was a good sign. It meant she was holding her own. But there was something so vulnerable about the fragile figure in the bed, hanging on so desperately to the thin thread of life. The X-rays had been taken that

afternoon and had confirmed that there was con-
siderable swelling of the brain, just as Drew had
said. As she went off duty Sandie popped her head
round the door of Sister's office. The night sister
had come on at eight o'clock. Marion Clarke was
quite young, not much older than Sandie herself,
and she liked her very much.

'I hope she'll still be here when I come on in the
morning,' Sandie said wistfully, glancing back towards Donna's bed. Sister Clarke looked at her
reprovingly.

'What kind of talk is that? I hope you're not
going to allow yourself to become too involved,
Staff. I'm sure you know the folly of that.'

Sandie gave her a wry look. 'You haven't met her
mother yet,' she said cryptically.

She was crossing the forecourt on her way to the
nurses' home when she heard a car hooting at her.
Looking round she saw Drew pulling up beside her.
He wound down the window.

'Come for a coffee?'

She looked down at her uniform. 'Like this? I've
only just come off duty.'

'Go and get a coat,' he commanded. 'I'll wait.'

She hesitated. Her feet ached and she wore no
make-up. Her hair hadn't been combed since
breakfast and she knew she looked far from her
best. But one look at his face sent her scurrying
towards the nurses' home. It was a chance to see
him—to be with him. Even if it was only for a few
minutes, it was worth it.

As she slipped into the car beside him ten minutes later, her hair brushed out and fresh lipstick
applied, he smiled.

'That was quick. Is there anywhere special you'd like to go?'

She glanced at him, moistening her lips. 'Could we go to the flat?'

He shook his head firmly. 'I think not. I know a quiet little pub where they serve good coffee. I can't have anything stronger tonight in case I'm called for an emergency op.'

'On Donna, you mean?' she looked at him. 'How long before you can diagnose her, do you think?'

He shook his head. 'Impossible to say. When the oedema has reduced I shall know more.'

'Will she be all right?'

'She's a strong child. I'm sure the odds are with her.'

She glanced at him. 'You handled her step-mother well.'

He opened his mouth to reply, then thought better of it and closed it again, remaining silent until they drew up in the car park of a small hotel on the outskirts of Hartmoor. Inside there was a re-laxed, cosy atmosphere. A log fire burned in the inglenook fireplace and the landlord, a cheerful, red-faced man, greeted Drew warmly.

'Good evening, Doctor. What can I get you? Your usual whisky and soda, or are you on duty?'

'I am. Just coffee for me, thank you, Frank. But I'm sure the young lady would like something stronger.' He looked at her enquiringly but Sandie shook her head.

'Coffee will be fine for me too, thanks.'

They took their cups over to the fireplace and sat down. Drew looked at her. 'You must be wonder-ing about the scene in the corridor this afternoon.'

'Not really,' she lied. 'Anyway, it's none of my business, is it?'

'Eve and I met a long time ago,' he told her. 'It was during my year at music college. She was all set for a career in opera in those days, but she changed her mind when she had the offer of a part in a West End musical. As it happened, she made the right decision. She hasn't looked back since.'

'And Donna's father?' she asked.

'He was an American businessman. He was killed in an air crash two years ago. Didn't you read about it in the papers?'

Sandie shook her head. 'No, I didn't. What were they doing here in Hartmoor?'

'Visiting a relative, apparently.' Drew stirred his coffee thoughtfully. 'Eve is a very highly-strung woman,' he said at last. 'I suppose it's to be expected in her profession.'

'Were you and she close?' Sandie ventured, looking into her cup.

'Once, many years ago,' he admitted. 'We were both very young at the time. We lost touch after I left the college to study medicine.'

'She had no trouble recognising you again,' Sandie said reflectively. 'They say one never forgets one's first love.'

His hand covered hers as it lay on the table and she looked up to find him looking at her. 'Sandie, you know as well as I do that we're totally unsuited to one another, don't you?' he said quietly.

Her heart gave a painful lurch. 'Are you telling me that you don't want to see me again? You don't have to wrap it up, you know. I've told you before, I'm not a child.'

His fingers tightened round hers. 'I couldn't say I didn't want to see you again without being a liar.' He glanced round. The room was beginning to fill up. 'Let's get out of here,' he said.

It was almost dark outside and in the shadows of the car park he pulled her close, stroking her hair and whispering her name. 'Sandie, darling, please don't look like that. I wouldn't have you hurt for the world. If only you didn't feel things so deeply.'

She swallowed the threatening tears. 'I don't usually,' she said painfully. 'It's just that I love—' He put his fingers over her lips.

'No! Don't say it. Oh, it isn't that I don't want to hear it. Just that I don't deserve to. I blame myself so much for making you unhappy, but I don't know what I can do about it.'

'I do,' she murmured, her head against his shoulder.

He kissed her forehead. 'If you only knew how hard it is at this moment not to give in.' He sighed. 'Come on. I'll take you home.'

In the car she glanced at his profile. 'Why did you ask me to have coffee with you this evening? Was it just to tell me you didn't want to see me again, or to explain about Eve?'

He turned to her with a wry smile. 'An older woman would never have asked that question,' he told her. 'And a younger man wouldn't tell you the answer.'

'Well—what *is* the answer?' she asked defiantly.

He switched on the ignition and nosed the car out of the car park on to the road before replying. 'The answer, my darling child, is that when I saw you crossing the hospital forecourt this evening, with your cap slightly awry and your shoulders drooping with tiredness, I just couldn't resist it. Wanting to take care of you is getting to be a habit—one which I must learn to break myself of.'

She looked despairingly at his features—the determined set of his mouth that she was beginning to know and dread.

'But why?' she demanded. 'I can't see why!'

He turned the car into the quiet road next to the hospital, a few yards from the entrance to the nurses' home. Switching off the engine he turned to her, one arm along the back of her seat.

'I told you that Eve and I were at music college together,' he said. 'I was twenty then. Do you realise how old you were?' Before she could reply he went on, 'You were three—a babe in arms. Seeing Eve today brought it home to me more than ever. That's why I had to talk to you this evening.'

The hurt inside Sandie welled up, making her want to lash out, to hurt him as much as he was hurting her. 'And what *else* did it bring back, seeing Eve? You might as well be honest about your reason for wanting to brush me off!' Her eyes were bright with tears and he grasped her shoulders.

'Sandie! Stop that. You don't know what you're saying. If you only knew how I—' He broke off, stiffening, as a uniformed figure passed the car, giving them a curious look. Following his glance, Sandie recognised Jenny Sammes.

'I'd better go,' she said miserably. 'Talking isn't getting us anywhere, is it?' And without waiting for his reply she got out of the car, running in through the entrance doors before he could call her back.

CHAPTER SIX

JENNY WAS waiting for the lift. She turned, giving Sandie a speculative look. 'Oh, it *was* you then? I thought I must have been mistaken.'

'Yes, it was me,' Sandie said noncommittally. The lift arrived and they got in. Jenny pressed the button for their floor, glancing at Sandie with concern.

'Are you all right? You look absolutely shattered. Fed up, too. Anything wrong?'

Sandie swallowed hard. 'No—well, we had this little girl admitted this morning. A traffic accident case. It's touch and go.'

Jenny's face brightened. 'Oh yes, I heard about it. Eve Paul's child, isn't it?'

Sandie pulled a face. 'Bad news travels fast!'

'Well you know what the hospital grape-vine is. And we don't often get to see any celebrities here.'

Sandie sighed, getting out of the lift as it stopped. 'You can think yourself lucky in this case.'

'Temperamental, is she? I did hear there'd been a bit of a scene up in IC. Someone said that the only person who could calm her was Maxie. Is it true?'

'Yes, it's true,' Sandie said wearily, inserting her key in the door.

Jenny looked at her expectantly. 'Got time for a coffee and a natter? I'll make it if you want to put your feet up.'

'Look, I'm sorry, but I can't tell you any more.'

As soon as she had said it Sandie was sorry. Jenny's bright, open face dropped in surprise and she turned away.

'Sorry, I only thought—'

'Please, don't go. I'd love to have a chat and a coffee, Jenny. I didn't mean to snap at you like that.' Sandie opened the door and held it for Jenny. 'Come in. I'm afraid it's been one of those days.'

She filled the kettle and plugged it in while Jenny perched on the end of her bed.

'Look, tell me to mind my own business if you like, but were you getting into hot water with Maxie out there just now? It looked a bit, well— fraught.'

Sandie sighed and dropped into a chair. Jenny's pretty, bright face was sincere. She wasn't just curious, looking for a nice juicy bit of gossip. And Sandie badly needed someone to talk to.

'I've just made a prize fool of myself,' she said.

'In what way?'

'The usual way. I fell in love.'

Jenny put her head on one side. 'With Maxie, you mean. So what's unusual about that? Everyone does it.'

Sandie smiled ruefully. 'Yes, but the difference between me and everyone else is that *they* keep it to themselves!'

Jenny frowned. 'I don't quite see. I thought you and he had got off to such a bad start . . .'

Sandie got up to pour water into the two mugs and add instant coffee. 'We did. The accidents just went on and on until it became so ludicrous that there was nothing else for it but to laugh. He asked me out to dinner and—well, one thing led to another. I suppose I must have taken it all too seriously.'

Jenny wrapped her hands round her mug and settled herself more comfortably. 'How do you mean exactly?'

Sandie bit her lip. 'I read too much into what he said and—and did,' she said awkwardly. 'I was vain enough to think he felt more than friendship.'

Jenny snorted. 'What you're saying is that he tried it on and when he found you weren't a push-over he brushed you off!' She rolled her eyes ceiling-wards. 'Huh! The same old story.'

'Oh no! It wasn't like that at all!' Sandie said quickly. 'What he says is that the age difference is too much.'

The other girl looked at her pityingly. 'Oh, can't you see, love? He's trying to let you down lightly. If I were you I'd forget all about him.'

'That's easy to say,' Sandie said unhappily. 'I'm beginning to wish I'd never come to Hartmoor General to work!'

'Now, now, we can't have that kind of talk!' Jenny reached out to squeeze her arm. 'Look, there's an informal party thing going on this evening over at The Feathers. Why don't you come across with me after you've had a bath and a bite to eat?'

Sandie shook her head. 'I couldn't. I'm too tired and I'm hardly in a party mood. I'd just put a damper on the whole thing.'

'No you wouldn't,' Jenny told her firmly. 'I refuse to leave you here moping, so there. I'll be back for you in about an hour—right?'

Sandie hesitated. She really didn't feel like it, but

on the other hand the alternative, her own company, was worse. At last she agreed.

The small bar at The Feathers was crowded with nurses and medical students. Sandie recognised one or two housemen and Tommy Bryant, Drew's young registrar. She hung back a little and Jenny pushed her forward.

'Go on. It's every man for himself at these dos. Strictly sex-equality. No use expecting any of the men here to offer to buy you a drink!' She glanced at Sandie. 'I don't know though, you look positively sparkling now that you've had time to collect yourself. I knew you wouldn't let old Maxie get you down!'

But Sandie knew that most of the sparkle was due to the contents of her make-up bag. It was amazing what a little blusher and eyeshadow could do for her appearance and confidence, both of which were sadly in need of a boost. Trying to decide what to wear, she had chosen an angora sweater in a soft turquoise shade, and teamed it with a slim black skirt. Jenny spotted a couple of vacant chairs and pushed Sandie into one of them.

'Here, watch these like a hawk while I get us a drink. What will you have, lager?'

'Tomato juice will be fine for me,' Sandie said, sitting down gratefully and putting her handbag on the other chair. It was hot and crowded—noisy too, as someone began to play the ancient upright piano in the corner. Jenny vanished among the jostling throng at the bar and Sandie gave a sigh, hoping they wouldn't stay too long.

'Well, hallo there! Not drinking? We can't have that, can we?' Sandie looked up to see Tommy

Bryant smiling down at her. It was the first time she had seen him without a white coat and she was surprised to see how much younger he looked in jeans and a sweater.

'It's all right. My friend is getting me a tomato juice, thanks,' she told him.

He pulled a face. 'Tomato juice? What kind of a drink is that to celebrate anyone's birthday?'

'I didn't know it was anyone's birthday. I wasn't invited—someone said it was informal.'

'So it is, so it is.' He removed her bag from the other chair and sat down on it, leaning towards her. He was a good-looking young man with a shock of brown curly hair and bright blue eyes. His long, mobile mouth always seemed about to laugh. He was very popular with nurses and patients alike; in fact he could even make Sister Milton laugh. He looked at her earnestly.

'Now, if I had known you were free I'd have invited you myself. I just didn't think there was a chance of you accepting!' The blue eyes twinkled wickedly behind thick lashes.

'You mean it's *your* birthday?' When he nodded she blushed and said, 'Oh, many happy returns. I wish someone had told me.'

'Really? What would you have done? Brought me a present?' His lips curved mischievously. 'Never mind. Tell you what, I'll settle for a birthday kiss.' He leaned forward, closing his eyes and puckering his lips, but at that moment Jenny arrived, hot and flustered, carrying two glasses. She nudged his shoulder with her hip.

'Off that chair, Bryant! Sandie was saving it for me.'

He opened his eyes to gaze into Sandie's. 'Is that really your name? Not because of your hair, surely? It's more the colour of autumn leaves.'

Jenny pulled a face as she handed Sandie her drink. 'Skip the poetry, Tommy. It makes you sound like a prize idiot. And give me that chair. Where are your manners?'

He glanced up at her. 'Haven't you heard, we're all equal now!' He rose reluctantly and stood grinning down at her. 'Still, never let it be said that I had no finer feelings. How could I refuse a seat to someone as haggard-looking as you!'

With a wink at Sandie he melted into the crowd and Jenny took his place, quite unperturbed by the scathing remark. Sandie stared at her.

'Are you always that rude to each other?'

Jenny laughed. 'Tommy and I have had this love-hate thing going for years. We grew up in the same road and I've known him since ever—worse luck. I hope he wasn't trying to chat you up. He can't resist trying out his so-called charm on every female he sees. I tell him it's a sign of insecurity.'

Sandie laughed and sipped her tomato juice. 'It's very warm in here,' she began, but at that moment a group of young people stopped beside them and one of them seized Jenny by the arm.

'There you are! We've been looking everywhere for you! We're going on to a disco—coming with us?' The girl who had spoken smiled at Sandie. 'Would you like to come too?'

Jenny swallowed the last of her drink and stood up. 'Great! It's not exactly swinging in here, is it?' She looked at Sandie. 'Coming?'

Sandie shook her head. 'I think I'll get an early

night, if you don't mind. It's been quite a day, one way and another.'

Jenny shook her head and bent to speak into Sandie's ear. 'Where's your spirit? Show him you don't give a damn! Come on, it'll do you good.'

But Sandie remained firm. 'No. You go, Jenny. I'll see you tomorrow. I really do feel tired.'

'Sure you'll be all right?' Jenny looked concerned.

'Of course. I'll just finish my drink, then wander back to the nurses' home. You go and have a good time. I'm fine.'

When they had gone she tossed back the last of her drink and got to her feet. A group of people were singing raucously round the piano now and she made her way across the room, skirting the crowd carefully. But just as she was pushing the door open a voice spoke at her side.

'You're not leaving already, are you?'

She turned to find herself looking into Tommy Bryant's blue eyes. 'I was, yes.'

'Oh, that's too bad. I was hoping for a chance to get to know you better. Aren't you enjoying my party?'

'It isn't that. I'm rather tired. We've had a heavy day on Intensive Care.'

He cocked an eyebrow at her. 'Mmm, battle fatigue. As your personal physician I prescribe a large dose of relaxation. Doesn't do to take one's work home, you know.'

She smiled. 'I don't usually.'

His hand closed warmly round her arm. 'It's that kid, isn't it? Somehow they always get to us, whether we admit it or not. Little perishers.' He bent to look into her eyes. 'Cheer up. Let me get you another drink, something a bit more uplifting.'

'No thanks.'

'How about some elixir of Bryant?' He kissed his fingertips. 'Chateau-bottled at great expense in the sunny vineyards of Hartmoor. Worth its weight in gold!' When she turned a pair of enquiring green eyes up to his, he laughed. 'I'm talking about my scintillating company, sweetheart! Well, if there's nothing else I can do for you, at least let me walk you home?'

'But I couldn't allow you to leave your own party,' she protested as he took her arm.

He laughed. 'This lot wouldn't notice me now if I took all my clothes off and walked across the ceiling! I might as well do what I want. After all, it is my birthday, and I happen to want to walk you home—right?'

The night was clear and moonlit as they walked across the road towards the nurses' home, but the air had grown chilly and Sandie shivered a little after the heat of the bar. Immediately Tommy's arm draped itself warmly across her shoulders and pulled her snugly against his side.

'Never think it was June, would you? You know, it was a bit of luck, young Jenny bringing you across tonight. I've been looking for an excuse to get to know you and this was the perfect opportunity.' He grinned down at her. 'You may not believe it, but I'm actually very shy.'

She laughed out loud and he joined in. 'Hey, that's better! I was beginning to think you couldn't do that.' He stopped walking and pulled her round to face him. 'I wonder if you have any idea what a difference it makes to you when you smile. You're pretty when you don't, but when you do you're positively beautiful!'

She raised an eyebrow. 'And you claim that you're shy?'

'Oh, I am,' he insisted seriously. 'It attacks people in different ways, you know. Some try to merge into the wallpaper but I tend to show off to cover mine. It's all a question of simple psychology.'

Privately Sandie thought it was all a question of shooting a line, but she kept the theory to herself. There was something very likeable about Tommy Bryant, and at this moment his brash cheerfulness was just what she needed to revive her flagging spirits.

'I suppose a girl like you is bound to have a steady boyfriend,' he said conversationally. 'If not a whole string of them.'

She shook her head. 'I haven't been here long. There *was* someone—at least I thought there was, until . . .' she trailed off as he squeezed her shoulders.

'Say no more. You are looking at someone very experienced in the art of picking up the pieces. For some strange reason no girl ever seems to take me seriously. They just don't understand how tender and vulnerable I am. My heart has been broken so many times it must look like a jigsaw puzzle!'

Sandie gave him a wry smile. 'I don't think I quite believe that!'

He lifted his shoulders. 'There you are, that's the story of my life. I'm dreadfully misunderstood. Now, you look to me like the kind of girl who likes helping lame dogs over stiles and that sort of thing. How about taking me on? I'm the lamest dog you ever saw!'

She looked up at him and laughed, unable to think of anything less lame-looking. 'The only time I tried to help a lame dog it bit me,' she said, borrowing his metaphor.

He turned a shocked face towards her. 'You surely don't think that I'd do a thing like that?' He grinned impishly. 'At least, not without encouragement!'

They had reached the doors of the nurses' home now and Sandie felt suddenly exhausted. She turned to him.

'Thank you for seeing me home. Goodnight.'

He grasped her shoulders. 'Don't I get invited up for a coffee?'

She shook her head. 'Sorry, no. Perhaps some other time.'

He looked into her eyes, his own serious. 'You really are worried about that child, aren't you? Tell you what, would you like me to go up to IC and check on her? You can come too if you like.'

She smiled. 'Oh, would you really? But your party?'

'Blow the party. It was a bore anyway. If I can bring the sparkle back to those beautiful green eyes—'

He took her hand firmly in his and together they walked across the forecourt to the hospital. Everywhere was quiet as they went up in the lift and as they walked along the corridor towards Intensive Care, Sandie was acutely aware of every footfall on the tiled floor. Tommy tapped gently on the door of Sister's office, then put his head round it.

'Thought I'd just pop in and take a look at the little Fenning girl, Sister,' he said. 'How is she?'

Sister Clarke looked up in surprise. 'Mr Maxwell has just this minute been in. It's a wonder you didn't see him on your way in. Donna's still holding her own, there's no change.' She caught sight of Sandie standing behind Tommy and her eyebrows rose. 'Ah, I see why you're here now! Sandie, what are you doing here? You should be getting your rest.'

'She was at my birthday party but she couldn't relax,' Tommy explained. 'I thought a look at Donna might put her mind at rest.' He slipped an arm round Sister's waist, his eyes devouring her exaggeratedly. 'And of course, I couldn't resist a chance to catch a glimpse of the most delicious sister in the hospital.'

Sister Clarke shrugged him off. 'Well, now that both of you have satisfied your curiosity you can make yourselves scarce,' she said unsmilingly. 'You know quite well that off-duty wanderings are not encouraged.'

On the way down in the lift Tommy looked at Sandie, shaking his head. 'See what I mean about being misunderstood?' He smiled. 'Do you feel happier about your patient now?'

She nodded. 'Yes, thank you.'

The lift stopped and they got out. Sandie looked at him. 'Please, go back to your party now. I can easily take myself across to the nurses' home.'

He looked down at her uncertainly. 'Do I get to see you again?'

She smiled. 'I don't see how it can be avoided, seeing that we work in the same building.'

'Come on, you know what I mean.'

In the silent, dimly lit corridor, he stopped and put his hands on her shoulders. 'I'm terribly disappointed. You're not going to send me away like this, are you? On my birthday, too?' The blue eyes sparkled with mischief as he bent his head and brushed his lips across hers. Then he wrapped his arms around her and kissed her very thoroughly. Suddenly the silence was broken by the sound of a door opening quite close to them. Sandie pushed Tommy away from her in a panic.

'Goodnight, Bryant,' she heard a voice say.

Startled, she spun round to find herself looking straight into Drew's eyes. They were as cold as stone. She felt her cheeks turning scarlet, but Tommy was quite unruffled.

'Ah, do you know Staff Nurse Sandie here? She was just wishing me a happy birthday,' he said.

'So I noticed,' Drew said dryly, and continued on his way down the corridor.

Tommy slipped his arms around her again but she shrugged him off.

'I must go now, please.'

He laughed. 'It's all right. He's gone. Anyway, he's quite broad-minded.'

'I want to go. I'm tired.' Sandie was close to tears and she wanted the privacy of her own room.

'All right. You haven't said yet when you'll see me again.' He hurried at her side as she made for the main entrance.

'I don't know. Please leave me alone now, Tommy. I've had enough for one day.' She hurried away into the darkness, leaving him staring after her, bewildered that she should be so embarrassed at being caught flirting in this day and age.

Closing the door of her room behind her at last, Sandie leaned against it and let out her breath in a long sigh. What a disastrous day! She undressed quickly, cleaned off her make-up and climbed gratefully into bed, snapping out the bedside light and watching the tossing patterns made on the ceiling by the trees outside. If only she didn't feel things so deeply. If only she hadn't fallen in love with Drew. Why couldn't she have chosen someone carefree and uncomplicated like Tommy? She thought of his snatched kiss and realised that it had hurt something deep inside her—given her a sense of loss and an aching longing that was almost unbearable. She wondered what Drew had thought when he saw Tommy kissing her. Had he minded— been jealous? Or had he simply felt a sense of release?

She turned over and punched her pillow savagely. If she didn't get to sleep soon she would be worse than useless tomorrow. She closed her eyes. But in the darkness of her mind she saw Eve Paul sobbing in Drew's arms and heard again the words he had spoken to her earlier that evening . . . 'Sandie, you know as well as I do that we're totally unsuited to each other.' The sentence had such a final ring to it.

CHAPTER SEVEN

DREW TOOK the decision to operate on Donna Fenning the following morning. He left a message for Sister Milton to send for him as soon as the child's stepmother arrived. When Sandie came on duty she discovered to her surprise that Eve Paul had been asking for her.

There was a definite edge to Sister's voice as she told her,

'It seems that you made quite an impression on her yesterday and she wants you to go and hold her hand! She's in the waiting-room.'

It was unlike Sister Milton to take this attitude towards a relative and Sandie looked at her in surprise.

'No need to look at me like that, Staff,' Sister said defensively. 'I know she's the child's step-mother, but I pride myself on being a good judge of character and I see trouble there!' She cleared her throat and brushed an imaginary speck from her skirt. 'Well, I suppose you'd better run along and minister to her before she starts complaining again!'

Eve sat in the waiting-room, her fur coat thrown carelessly over the arm of her chair. She looked up when Sandie came in, her large, expressive eyes brimming with anxious tears.

'Ah, there you are. Sandie, isn't it? Apart from Drew you're the only *humane* person in the place!

When I arrived there was a scene down in reception about the Press.'

'The Press?' Sandie asked, puzzled.

'Yes. News travels fast you know, especially bad news. It isn't my fault that they want the story, is it? It isn't exactly pleasant, having them cash in on one's grief.' She looked at Sandie apprehensively. 'I hardly dare ask you, but what does Drew want to see me about?'

Sandie sat down beside her. 'He's told you that he wants to operate?'

Eve nodded. 'I was told there is some form or other that I have to sign.' She sighed. 'I wouldn't say this to many people, Sandie, but I'm terrified of the responsibility. She isn't even my own child, you see. What if something were to go wrong? I'd never forgive myself.'

'But you are her next of kin,' Sandie said gently. 'The only person who can take that responsibility.' For the first time she felt sorry for Eve. Suddenly the facade of glamour dropped and she looked unsure of herself—almost as vulnerable as Maddie had been. 'I'm sure you have every confidence in Mr Maxwell,' she said reassuringly. 'When he gets here he'll put you in the picture, then you'll feel much better about it, I'm sure. In the meantime, would you like to go and sit with Donna for a while? I'll come and fetch you as soon as Mr Maxwell gets here.'

But Eve shook her head. 'I can't bear to see her lying there like that. Anyway, she wouldn't even know I was there, would she?'

'No one ever really knows that for sure,' Sandie told her. 'Sometimes, it helps to talk to the patient.'

But Eve shook her head again.

'No, perhaps when I've spoken to Drew.'

At that moment the door opened and he came in, his handsome face grave. Sandie's heartbeat quickened as he greeted them both formally.

'Good morning.' He looked at Sandie. 'Thank you, Staff. You can go back to the ward now.' But Eve grasped her hand and clung to it.

'No, I'd like Sandie to stay, if you don't mind, Drew. She's been so kind. At times like this there's nothing quite like the support of another woman.'

Sandie saw Drew's eyebrows rise slightly but he said nothing. Sitting down beside Eve he looked at her candidly. 'I would like to operate on Donna as soon as possible,' he told her. 'Now that the internal swelling has reduced I find that the bleeding caused by her injury has formed a clot which is at present pressing on the brain. It is important that the pressure is relieved at once.'

'Is that why she's still unconscious?' Eve asked in a whisper.

'Partly, yes.'

Eve stifled a sob. 'And afterwards, if there is an afterwards, will she be crippled. A *vegetable*?'

Sandie saw Drew wince at the choice of words before he said patiently, 'She's a strong child with a healthy constitution and the vital signs are encouraging, but I shall be able to tell you more after the operation.' He produced the consent form. 'If you could sign here.' He took a pen from his pocket and handed it to her. For a moment she looked at him with huge, bewildered eyes, then signed her name with a flourish. As she handed back the pen she sighed.

'Oh dear. I only hope I'm doing the right thing.'

'Believe me, you're doing the only thing,' Drew said as he got to his feet. He touched her shoulder. 'Try not to worry. I'll do everything I can. Would you like to sit with her a while? I'm sure Sister won't mind.' But Eve shook her head.

'I can't bear to see her lying there like that, wired up to those awful machine things.'

'Then go home and try to get some rest,' Drew advised. 'I'll be in touch as soon as she's out of the theatre.' He looked at Sandie. 'Perhaps you'd be kind enough to see Miss Paul back to her car, Staff.' For a moment their eyes met and Sandie looked eagerly for some sign—a smile, or a flicker of warmth. But he looked at her coolly, as though she were a stranger. She nodded, avoiding his eyes.

'Of course.'

On the way down in the lift Eve confessed that she was relieved that Drew had come to a decision. She clung to Sandie's arm as they crossed the lobby, but as they walked out on to the forecourt together Sandie was suddenly blinded as a battery of photographers rushed forward, flashing their cameras at them. To her amazement, Eve responded immediately by straightening her shoulders and flashing a brave smile. A reporter stepped forward.

'Can you tell us the latest news about your daughter, Miss Paul?' Another jostled him.

'Has she regained consciousness? Are they going to operate?'

A woman reporter cast a speculative eye over Sandie. 'Are you the nurse who is looking after her? Can we have your angle? What it is like to nurse the child of a celebrity? Something on those lines.'

But Sandie backed away, shaking her head. 'No, I'm sorry, I have to go.' She glanced towards Eve for support, but the singer was surrounded by reporters and a photographer blocked Sandie's view. As she hurried back to the ward she thought about Eve and her stepdaughter. It couldn't be easy to put on a brave face under circumstances like that. Everyone naturally assumed that Eve was playing to the gallery, but this morning Sandie had seen another side of her—a more caring side that had filled her with compassion. Certainly Eve had switched on a smile for the Press, but then that was part of her training. It didn't necessarily mean she had no feelings. We were all what life made of us, after all.

It was almost supper time before Donna Fenning came back from theatre. Sandie sat by her bed, watching the small, still figure, looking for the slightest change. The report was good; there had been no irreparable damage. Everything now depended upon the child's resilience and ability to heal. At eight o'clock Tommy Bryant came up to see her. He made a brief examination and nodded to Sandie.

'She's doing fine. You look all in. Shouldn't you be off duty by now?'

She glanced at her watch. 'I will be soon.' She looked down at Donna. 'I've been hanging on, hoping she might come round before I went off.'

He shook his head. 'It'll be some hours yet.' He glanced round to satisfy himself that Sister wasn't within hearing. 'Look, Sandie, I'm sorry if I embarrassed you last night,' he said.

She smiled. 'It's all right.'

'Have dinner with me later and let me make it up to you?' His blue eyes twinkled hopefully at her.

She hesitated. 'Well, I don't know—'

'I've got something to show you, a surprise,' he said temptingly.

'What can that be?'

'I can't tell you now. Tell you what, I'll bring it over later—right?'

She lifted her shoulders resignedly. 'All right then, half-past nine.'

Tommy was as good as his word, arriving dead on the stroke of the half-hour. He wore his off-duty clothes, jeans and a sweater, and carried a paper carrier bag bearing the name of the local Chinese take-away. Under his arm was a folded newspaper and Sandie reflected that he looked as though he was prepared for a siege. She couldn't help smiling as she let him in and he held up the paper bag.

'You see, I've forestalled your protests by bringing dinner with me!'

'Very far-sighted,' she said dryly.

'Think nothing of it. I get these flashes of genius from time to time,' he said with an airy wave of the hand. 'Now, where are the plates and cutlery?'

She fetched them and he dished up the food deftly. As he handed her plate he suddenly remembered something.

'Oh, I almost forgot. Here is the surprise I told you about.' He picked up the newspaper and opened it with a flourish. There, on the front page, was a photograph of herself and Eve emerging from the hospital that morning. Underneath was the caption, *Hartmoor Angel ministers to singing star!* Below was a report of Donna's accident and progress, complete with dramatic embellishments. Eve had obviously done them proud! Tommy grinned at her.

'What do you think of that? Fame at last, eh?'

She stared at him in horror. 'Oh no! This is going to make me *very* popular! It looks as though I pushed myself forward when all the time I was trying to get away!'

Tommy laughed. 'Eve Paul doesn't share your horror of the limelight. Who was it who said that bad publicity was preferable to no publicity? I'd say she was using her stepdaughter's accident to revive her flagging popularity.'

'I think that's very unkind of you!' Sandie retorted. 'Anyway, it wasn't even my idea to escort her to her car,' she added. 'Mr Maxwell asked me to go down with her.'

Tommy looked at her sharply. 'Then he'll know not to blame you, won't he? Why do you care so much about what he thinks? You haven't got a *thing* about him, have you?'

She felt her cheeks redden. 'None of your business!'

He put down his knife and fork to stare at her. 'Good Lord, I do believe you have! Forget him, sweetheart. He's old enough to be your father!'

'Hardly, at thirty-nine!' she retorted.

He narrowed his eyes at her. 'Ah, you *have* been doing your homework, haven't you? No wonder you were so upset that he caught us kissing in the corridor last night.' He chuckled. 'No need to worry, poppet. Drew is like measles or acne—all the young nurses in this hospital get a bout of him at some time or another. It's part of growing up!' He assumed his 'doddering professor' voice. 'Symptoms may resemble those of a broken heart but they are primarily psychosomatic. Treatment—removal of patient from cause, as for allergy.' He grinned wickedly at her. 'Large doses of concentrated Bryant have proved effective in certain cases.'

Sandie got to her feet, irritated by his schoolboyish brand of humour. 'Not in this case though.' She began to clear away the dishes. 'Look, Tommy, I shall have to throw you out now.'

His smile vanished as he stood up to face her. 'Oh, come on, Sandie! Where's your sense of humour?'

'When I'm with you it seems to suffer from bouts of amnesia,' she told him tartly, then relented at his crestfallen face. 'It was sweet of you to bring supper for me. I did enjoy it, honestly, but I want to wash my hair and—'

He held up his hand. 'All right, you don't have to spell it out for me. I've made you cross. That's my trouble, I tend to go over the top.' He put his hands on her shoulders. 'But I shall return!' he announced dramatically. 'To woo you with wine and roses in the manner you deserve.'

She smiled in spite of herself. 'You're an idiot, Tommy Bryant.'

His smile returned. 'I find that distinctly encouraging. I'm not easily put down, you see. I believe that's one of my greatest charms.' He looked into her eyes. 'Would you believe me if I told you that being close to you like this made my back teeth ache?'

She laughed. 'I refuse to be drawn on that one. Now, will you please go?'

He kissed her lightly. 'I must be mad, wasting my time with you when there are girls out there wasting away for love of me. I think I must be falling in love.'

'Not you. You wouldn't know how to be that stupid!'

When he had gone Sandie cleared away the dishes and washed them up in the kitchen. She wished she could have Tommy's light-hearted attitude to life. Everything seemed such fun to him. If only she could share that outlook. She heard the telephone ring and a moment later Jenny put her head round the kitchen door.

'It's for you.'

As Sandie dried her hands the other girl looked at her. 'I saw Tommy Bryant leaving just now wearing a distinctly whipped look. It wouldn't have anything to do with you, would it?'

'We had a take-away meal together,' Sandie told her. 'But I had to throw him out afterwards. I wanted to wash my hair.'

Jenny laughed. 'That must have shaken him!'

'I didn't mean to hurt his feelings. I like him,' Sandie assured her. 'But he did invite himself up and he can be rather persistent.'

'That has to be the understatement of the year!' Jenny laughed. 'It will do him no harm at all to get the brush-off for once. No harm at all.'

When Sandie lifted the receiver she found

Madeleine at the other end of the line. She was bubbling over with excitement.

'Darling, I've just seen the local paper! You know, the picture of you with Eve Paul. How fascinating for you!'

'Oh, that. Her stepdaughter had her operation this afternoon,' Sandie told her.

'Did she? I do hope she'll be all right. Such a worrying time for Eve. Did I ever tell you that I was at school with her?' Madeleine asked.

'No, you didn't.' Sandie wondered how many more people had shared Eve Paul's formative years.

'I was wondering,' Madeleine went on, 'whether she'd like to come and visit me. Sitting in some hotel room at a time like this must be terrible for her. It doesn't say which hotel in the paper—well, of course, it wouldn't. Can you give it to me, Sandie, so that I can ring her?'

'I'm sorry, Maddie, I'm afraid I can't,' Sandie said. 'I'm not allowed to pass on information like that outside the hospital.'

'No, I do see that.' There was a pause. Then Madeleine said, 'But surely, in a case like this? All I want to do is help, Sandie. I'm sure she'd be glad of a friend at a time like this. She could even come and stay here at Elm Court if she felt like it. I think you could use your own discretion, couldn't you?'

Reluctantly Sandie gave Madeleine the number and then spent the rest of the evening worrying about it. Deep inside, something told her she was going to regret it. Madeleine may have known Eve a long time ago but she was sure that the two of them had less than nothing in common now.

As soon as she went on duty the following morning, Sandie asked about Donna. Sister Milton looked at her reprovingly.

'There are other patients in this ward, Staff,' she said stiffly. 'I don't think I need remind you that I do not approve of favouritism.'

It was quite clear that she was in one of her moods and Sandie made a mental note to keep out of her way as much as possible. 'I only wondered if she had regained consciousness,' she said. 'After all, I have been specialling her.'

Sister sniffed. 'Her condition is stable and she is breathing unaided,' she said, sounding like an official report. 'And you had better continue to special her, considering your new status as the "Hartmoor Angel"!'

Sandie winced as she turned away. It was what she had expected and she didn't imagine that the reaction would begin and end with Sister Milton, either.

She found Donna still lying motionless and pale. She checked with the nurse who was about to go off duty and made the routine observations, but just as she was taking the child's pulse the eyelids fluttered. Sandie felt her heart quicken with anticipation as she bent and spoke Donna's name softly. The little girl's eyes opened. They were a soft, dark brown. A small tongue came out to moisten dry lips.

'Why am I in bed?' she whispered, her dark eyes widening with apprehension.

Sandie pressed her hand. 'It's all right. Lie still. You had a little accident, but you're all right now.'

The little girl frowned. 'Can I have a drink?'

'Not yet—soon.' Sandie swabbed the dry lips. 'Try to sleep now. Next time you wake you'll feel much better, just you wait and see.' The brown eyes closed and a moment later the child had drifted into a peaceful sleep. Sandie went to find Sister.

'Donna Fenning has recovered consciousness,' she told her.

'Right. I'll ring Mr Maxwell at once. Thank you, Staff.' Sister looked at her with the ghost of a smile and Sandie said,

'It wasn't my fault you know—that newspaper article. Mr Maxwell asked me to see Miss Paul back to her car and they were all there waiting, like vultures.'

Sister touched her arm. 'I know. I can imagine how it was. I'm sorry if I was a bit sharp with you. It's been one of those mornings.'

Drew came up to the ward about twenty minutes later. He examined Donna and questioned Sandie about her. Just as he had finished, Sister Milton was called to the telephone so Sandie walked to the door with him.

'I expect you'll be telephoning her stepmother with the good news,' she said. 'And no doubt she'll be wanting to have her transferred to the private wing as soon as possible.'

He nodded. 'You sound as though you'll miss her.'

She smiled. 'I have to admit that I wanted to be the one who was there when she came round. I hated to go off duty last night.'

'So Dr Bryant told me.' He hesitated as he looked at her, as though trying to make up his mind about something. Then he said, 'By the way, I must congratulate you on your choice.'

She stared at him, puzzled. 'I'm sorry?'

'I'm talking about Bryant,' he said, a slight edge to his voice. 'Just the type for you. I'm glad you were able to find him so quickly.'

She flushed. 'If you're talking about the other evening, it wasn't the way it looked! I—'

He smiled at her, his eyes flinty. 'You don't have to make excuses for enjoying yourself, especially not to me!'

She opened her mouth to reply, but at that moment Sister came out into the corridor, flustered and red-faced.

'I'm glad you're still here, Mr Maxwell. That was Miss Paul on the telephone. It seems she's been trying to get you. She wants to bring a photographer up here this afternoon. I'm sorry, I know she's a friend of yours, but I can't have my ward disrupted like that. It's quite unthinkable. The risk of infection alone—' She stopped as Drew held up his hand.

'I quite agree, Sister. I would have told her the same myself. Of course it's out of the question.'

Sister Milton took a deep, relieved breath. 'Yes. Well, I hope you'll explain that to her. She was really quite abusive to me on the telephone just now. I have quite enough to do without all this.'

Drew smiled at her placatingly. 'I think you'll find that as soon as Donna is well enough she will be transferred to the private wing. That will take the pressure off you.'

'Well, I'm sorry to say that it will!' Sister Milton pulled the corners of her mouth down disapprovingly as she hurried back to her office. Drew smiled wryly.

'Poor Sister. Having the stepdaughter of a celebrity in her ward is throwing her routine to the winds. Let's hope it won't be for long.'

Sandie glanced towards Sister's office. 'About what you were saying—Dr Bryant and I hardly know one another.'

'You seem to be losing no time in putting that right,' he said dryly, beginning to walk away.

'I told you, it wasn't the way it looked,' Sandie began. Drew stopped and looked down at her, his mouth taut.

'Let him show you how to laugh, Sandie, how to have fun. I'm sure he's an expert in those things. I told you there was someone like that waiting for you. You're much too young to get bogged down emotionally.'

She bit her lip hard to stop the tears from gathering in her eyes. It was hopeless. He didn't want her. He thought of her as a nuisance, a responsibility he could well do without, and it hurt. It hurt unbearably. She swallowed hard at the lump in her throat.

'All right,' she said huskily. 'Thank you for the advice. I'll try to remember it. What was it? Oh yes, laugh and have fun!'

He touched her arm. 'Sandie, don't. Don't be bitter.'

She turned from him without another word and walked back through the glass doors into the ward, her head held high.

Drew stood for a long moment looking after her, his expression enigmatic. Then he too turned and walked away towards the lift.

CHAPTER EIGHT

DONNA FENNING continued to make a good recovery and, as Drew had anticipated, her stepmother asked for her to be transferred to the private wing as soon as she was off the critical list. Sandie assumed that this was so that she would be able to visit whenever she wanted. She was completely unprepared however, for Eve's request that she should be transferred with Donna and continue to special her. When Sister Milton heard about it she sucked in her cheeks ominously.

'Of course she's doing it just to spite me!' she announced. 'Just what am I expected to do until Nurse Collins gets back, I'd like to know?'

But later that morning, after a lot of telephoning, it became clear that Staff Nurse Collins would be reporting back for duty the following Monday morning. No further arguments that Sister Milton could put up would hold water, much to her disgust, which put her in a worse mood than ever.

It was arranged that after her weekend break Sandie should transfer to the private wing and remain there until Donna was discharged. It seemed there was very little to be done about it.

One person at least was pleased with the news, and that was Donna herself. In the days that followed the operation she had grown very attached to Sandie and the prospect of taking her very own nurse with her when she moved filled her with delight.

On Thursday afternoon Madeleine telephoned to say that she had arranged her dinner party for Saturday evening.

'I've decided to keep it small,' she told Sandie. 'Only the two of us, Andrew Phillips, the local GP who you've met before, Eve and Drew.'

Sandie's heart sank as she imagined how uncomfortable it would be, making trivial small talk with Drew across the dinner table. 'I see,' she said without enthusiasm. 'So you managed to speak to Eve, then?'

'Yes, I did and she was so pleased to hear from me again after all these years. It's mainly for her that I'm having the party this weekend,' Madeleine told her. 'I thought it would make a welcome break for her.' She paused. 'You don't mind, do you, Sandie?'

'Of course not. It's your home. You're free to invite whoever you like,' Sandie said quickly. 'It's just that, having met her, I can't imagine you two having much in common.'

Madeleine laughed. 'Well, it's true that our life-styles are poles apart of course, but old school-friends always revert when they meet again, however long the interval. You should have heard us when we talked on the telephone. You'd have thought we were both fourteen again!'

'Well, that's fine. I'm glad.'

'Oh, Sandie, before I forget. I shall be a man short. Do you know anyone you could ask?'

'Why me?' Sandie asked. 'Surely it should be someone you know? Or I'm sure that Eve Paul knows plenty of men.' She bit her lip as she realised, too late, the tartness of the remark. There was a pause before Madeleine said,

'I just thought it might be nice for you to invite someone of your own age-group. After all, we're all older than you. I did ask Drew Maxwell to bring his sister, but he said he didn't think she'd be home this weekend.'

'Look, Maddie, perhaps it would be better if I didn't come to the party,' Sandie said unhappily.

'*Sandie!*' Madeleine sounded shocked. 'What is it, love? Is something wrong?'

'Of course not. It's just—' She broke off as her throat constricted.

'It's something to do with Drew, isn't it? Oh, darling, I did warn you. Look, don't say any more now. We'll talk when you come home. Now, surely there's someone you can invite? Think,' Madeleine said.

'Well, there is a young doctor, but he may not be free. I'll see what I can do.'

'That's better. Please try. If it's any comfort to you, Eve thinks you're a wonderful nurse. She must do to ask for you specially to nurse Donna, mustn't she?'

Sandie smiled wryly to herself. 'Yes, I suppose she must. Well, I'll see you on Saturday then, Maddie. Bye.'

After she hung up she had second thoughts about inviting Tommy Bryant to the dinner party. It might give him the wrong idea. On the other hand however, it would show Drew that she hadn't taken his rebuff too much to heart. Of course, it might well be that Tommy would be on duty on Saturday evening, especially as Drew was off. But when she met him in the corridor later he told her that he was free. He accepted her invitation delightedly, saying that he would leave Madeleine's address and telephone number so that he could be contacted if he were needed in an emergency.

'Your chief will be there,' Sandie warned. 'That won't inhibit you, will it?'

He laughed. 'Good heavens, no! Why should it? It'll be interesting to meet the fabulous Eve Paul on social terms—*and*, of course, to spend an evening in your company.' He grinned at her. 'Will you hold my hand under the tablecloth?'

'That could make eating rather difficult.' Sandie stepped neatly out of his way. 'We'll expect you around eight o'clock then.'

Before she caught the bus out to Upper Longden she went into town to buy herself something to wear for the party. In spite of what Maddie had said about the party being a small one, she had the impression that it was to be rather grand and she hadn't anything in her wardrobe that was suitable. She looked around for some time and finally chose a dress in a smoky lavender shade, with a tiny lace bodice and floaty chiffon skirt that swirled around her hips in a mass of tiny pleats. It was far more expensive than she had intended and as she boarded the bus Sandie was consumed with guilty defiance, looking forward to Maddie's party with even more apprehension than before.

When she arrived at Elm Court, Madeleine came to the door to greet her. She hugged her step-daughter warmly, searching her face with anxious eyes.

'Mrs Simmons is in the kitchen helping me to get ready for this evening,' she said, slipping her arm through Sandie's as they went upstairs. 'As you know, she doesn't usually come in on Saturdays but she kindly agreed to come and give me a hand with the vegetables.' She opened the door of Sandie's room and stood back. 'Well, what do you think?'

Sandie gasped. 'Oh, Maddie, it's beautiful!' The room had been redecorated in shades of lavender and blue. The walls were papered with a tiny flower print that was echoed in the curtains; the carpet was the deep blue of delphiniums and the bed and dressing-table wore flounced white muslin valances. Sandie found herself biting back the tears as she remembered how off-hand she had been on the telephone. 'Oh, it's *lovely*—I don't know what to say.'

Madeleine closed the door and pushed her gently into a chair. 'I'm so glad you like it. I think we should have a little talk, don't you?'

Sandie swallowed hard. 'There isn't really anything to talk about.'

'I think there is.' Madeleine looked at her, her brown eyes shrewd. 'Something has happened, hasn't it? Surely you can talk to me about it, Sandie?'

Sandie looked down at her hands. There were times when her stepmother seemed to see right into her mind. She knew it was impossible to keep her feelings about Drew from her any longer.

'It was as you said. I got hurt,' she admitted in a small voice. 'I fell in love with Drew.' She looked up at Madeleine. 'He was attracted to me too. I know he was. It was just that he had this thing about our ages. I'm sure I could have convinced him that it didn't matter if Eve hadn't come back into his life. That really finished everything.'

Madeleine reached out to touch her hand. 'Oh dear, I was so afraid of this. Eve told me, of course, that she and Drew were old friends from college days.' She pressed Sandie's fingers. 'I see now why you wanted to opt out of the party. Poor Sandie. But what about the young doctor you mentioned. Did you invite him?'

'Yes, and he says he'd love to come,' Sandie told her. 'His name is Tommy Bryant and he's Drew's registrar. I think you'll like him.'

'Do *you* like him?' Madeleine looked closely at her but Sandie shook her head impatiently.

'He's all right—good company, but so *juvenile*, Maddie, so—so, oh, I don't know.'

'You mean he isn't Drew?' Madeleine said softly. 'I know, darling, but you'll get over him. You must. I think you know that, don't you?' She looked at the dress bag that Sandie had thrown on to the bed. 'Is that a new dress? Aren't you going to show me? Is it for the party?'

Sandie helped with the rest of the preparations, busying herself so that she didn't have too much time to think about the coming ordeal. She helped Madeleine to lay the table with her best crystal and silver, arranged flowers and folded napkins, until at last it was time to dress.

Dr Andrew Phillips was the first to arrive. He was the smiling, middle-aged Scotsman whom Sandie had met at Elm Court a few weeks before. Tommy Bryant arrived a few minutes after him, looking attractive in formal clothes and charming Madeleine from the first moment they met. He eyed Sandie with candid admiration, whispering to her as she handed him a sherry,

'You look good enough to eat and I think your stepmother is stunning! Don't tell me we're getting food too?'

She laughed in spite of her quaking stomach and was still talking to Tommy and Dr Phillips when the doorbell rang and Madeleine slipped out to answer it. Sandie hadn't noticed her leaving the room, so that when she turned and saw Eve and Drew standing in the doorway it came as something of a shock. Eve wore a dazzling dress of glowing red silk which clung to her perfect figure like a second skin. Her hair shone like pale satin, drawn smoothly back to show off an exquisite pair of diamond earrings.

'Wow!'

Sandie heard Tommy's muffled exclamation, but she was looking at Drew, standing behind Eve, a head and shoulders taller. He looked so handsome in a dark suit and white shirt, but Sandie couldn't help noticing that his hand lingered on Eve's arm and the solicitous way he smiled down at her. She stole a glance at his face, her eyes mutely searching his, but he smiled back blandly, giving nothing away, acknowledging her as though she was the most casual acquaintance.

The meal that Madeleine had taken so much trouble over was a great success. As they ate, Eve talked of Donna's miraculous escape and her luck at being in such good hands. She looked up at Drew admiringly, insisting that her stepchild could not have had better treatment anywhere else in the world, until Drew protested that he had simply done his job as any other doctor would have done.

Under cover of the tablecloth Tommy nudged Sandie and later, as they were moving into the drawing-room to take their coffee, he whispered, 'If you ask me, Drew has got himself well and truly hooked this time! I've never seen a more determined look in a woman's eyes!' He chuckled. 'Nice work if you can get it, as they say!'

Sandie made no reply, biting back her irritation and the strong urge to retaliate, which she knew would only give away her feelings.

As they were drinking their coffee, Andrew Phillips asked Eve when she would be doing another television show. She looked up at him with a sigh.

'In the autumn. It's rather a pity, really. I had hoped to be able to take Donna on holiday to help her to recuperate, but I'm afraid it's going to be out of the question. I start rehearsals the week after next, you see.'

Madeleine looked up suddenly. 'I've just had the most marvellous idea! Why don't you and Donna move in here and stay while I'm away on my holiday? It's quiet and away from your public, Eve. It's a beautiful spot and there's certainly no shortage of doctors in the area!' She smiled at Andrew and Drew and Tommy. 'What do you say, Eve?'

'Oh, but your beautiful new home! Are you sure you want to fill it with strangers?' Eve asked doubtfully.

'You're not strangers! And I'd be glad of someone to occupy the place while I'm away. You'd be doing me a favour in a way,' Madeleine assured her. 'Please give it some thought.'

Eve reached for Drew's hand and squeezed it, her eyes misty as she looked at him.

'Did you hear that? Aren't I lucky to have such wonderful friends?' Then her eyes clouded. 'Oh, but what will Donna do while I'm away in London rehearsing? I had intended to take her with me and leave her with an au-pair or someone, but here—it's such a long way, isn't it? I may not be able to get back each night.'

There was a moment's silence, then Eve turned to look at Sandie. 'I don't suppose it would be possible for you to come and look after her, would it, Sandie? She looks on you as her special nurse, she adores you, you know. I wouldn't worry about leaving her overnight if I knew you were with her. And I'd pay you well, of course. What do you say?'

Sandie flushed as all eyes turned in her direction. 'Oh, I'm sorry, but I really don't see how I could. I haven't been at Hartmoor General for long and I'm not due for any time off.'

Eve frowned. 'I see. But would you like the job? I mean, if it could somehow be arranged, would you be willing to take it?'

Sandie shook her head. 'I don't see how! Of course I'd like to help—' She broke off as she saw Eve look appealingly at Drew.

'I'm sure there are strings that you could pull, aren't there, darling?' She covered his hand with hers.

Drew's eyes met Sandie's across the room as he said, 'I'm sure we can arrange something. Donna should certainly have a qualified nurse with her if she is to be left for long periods.'

Sandie felt trapped. It was as though the whole thing was being taken out of her hands. She opened her mouth to say that she would like time to think about it, but at that moment the telephone rang. She jumped to her feet, glad of the diversion.

'It's all right, Maddie. I'll answer it.'

It was from the hospital, for Tommy. Sandie called him out into the hall to take it and a few minutes later he came back to confer with Drew.

'I'm afraid I shall have to leave,' he told Madeleine apologetically. 'It's a pity. I've enjoyed my evening so much.' He looked at Sandie. 'Are you going to walk out to the car with me?'

As they walked out on to the drive together Tommy slipped an arm round her waist. 'Thank you for inviting me this evening, Sandie. It's been very interesting. I had no idea that Drew and Eve were so—shall we say close?'

Sandie shrugged. 'Are they? I hadn't noticed.'

He squeezed her arm gently. 'Come off it. Anyone with half an eye could see that.' He stopped walking and looked at her. 'Oh, Sandie, you're not still carrying that particular torch, are you? Why waste your time when there are dashing young doctors like me around? Look at me. I've got youth on my side, a brilliant future, good looks—what more could a girl ask for? I'm even modest with it!' She laughed and he pulled her close. 'You look gorgeous tonight, Sandie. It's rotten luck, having to dash off like this. Come out with me again soon, eh?'

She hedged, trying to push him gently away. 'I don't know.'

He bent his head and kissed her swiftly. 'Mmm—

you know, of course, that playing hard to get is the biggest turn-on of all time, don't you?'

A sudden quiet voice behind them made Sandie jump. 'I'm sorry to intrude.' Drew's tall figure stepped out of the shadows. 'I just came out to say that if you have any doubts you can reach me here.' He was addressing Tommy, who turned to him without a flicker of embarrassment.

'Oh, fine. How long will you be staying?'

Drew looked at his watch. 'About another hour, I'd say. I'll be taking Eve back into Hartmoor and I'll look in at the hospital then, anyway. Goodbye.'

'Bye. See you, Sandie.' Tommy got into his car, turned his key in the ignition and a moment later was speeding down the drive. Sandie waved and went to walk back to the house, but Drew reached out to stop her, a hand on her arm.

'Sandie, wait. Before we go inside I'd like to speak to you.' She looked up at him. 'It's about the job that Eve offered you. If you'd like to take it I can arrange leave of absence for you.'

Sandie bit her lip, disappointment engulfing her that it was only work he wanted to talk about.. 'I haven't even had time to think about it yet,' she said.

His hand tightened on her arm. 'Then think about it now. I advise you to take it, Sandie.'

'Why?' She looked up at him.

His eyes clouded and avoided hers. 'I think it would be good for Donna. She's a lonely child and she needs the security of a stable relationship like the one she's built with you since she was admitted to Hartmoor General. Even though she can be discharged quite soon, she will still need skilled nursing and I'd be happier if you were with her.' His eyes sought hers again. 'It will be valuable experience for you, not just a glorified domestic job, if that's what is troubling you.'

Sandie flushed. The thought had crossed her mind that Eve thought of her more as a sort of nanny than a qualified nurse, and she was slightly ashamed of the idea. If the child needed her, of course she was willing to nurse her—whether here or at the hospital. She looked up at Drew hesitantly.

'Well, if you really think I should?'

'I do.' He looked searchingly at her. 'Of course, it may mean having to curtail your social life for a while.'

She coloured. Clearly he meant Tommy. 'It isn't important,' she said awkwardly. Suddenly she was acutely aware of his hand on her arm. It was as though a vital current flowed between them. Her heart quickened as she looked up at him. 'It isn't important, Drew. Surely you know that I—I don't—'

She broke off, the breath catching in her throat as he drew her towards him. In the semi-darkness she saw that the hard light in his eyes had softened. He was so close that she could feel the warmth and vitality of him, feel his breath on her cheek as he said quietly,

'Sandie, I want you to know, to *believe*, that I know what is best. I want—'

'Drew!' Eve's strident call cut through the stillness like a steel blade and Sandie turned to see her slim form silhouetted against the square of light at the top of the steps. She was peering out into the half-light, shielding her eyes as she called again.

'Drew! Are you out there? What are you doing?'

His arms dropped to his sides. 'I'm coming now!'

The moment was lost, contact between them severed, and as he began to walk towards the house Sandie followed, her heart heavy. Now she would never know what he had been about to say. Never have the chance to put her own side.

Tommy's departure seemed to unsettle the atmosphere of the party and soon afterwards it began to break up. First Dr Phillips took his leave, then a little later Eve declared that she was tired and asked Drew to take her home. When they had gone, waved off at the door by Madeleine, Sandie offered to help with the washing-up. Madeleine sank into a chair with a sigh.

'No, let's leave it. Mrs Simmons said she'd do it in the morning. It would be a pity to spoil a pleasant evening with a mundane job like washing-up, don't you think?' She glanced across at Sandie's pensive face. 'I like young Dr Bryant. He's fun. Oh, Sandie, I wish you wouldn't look so unhappy!'

Sandie looked up. 'Sorry. It's just that I feel I'm rather being pressured into taking time out to nurse Donna. I can't help wondering if Drew simply wants to get me away from the hospital for a while—out from under his feet!'

'Oh, surely not! After all, I presume he'll be coming here to see the child. He'll still come into contact with you anyway, won't he?'

Sandie nodded. 'I suppose so. On second thoughts, I doubt if he cares enough to go to those lengths to get me out of his life.'

Madeleine looked at the despairing face opposite her. 'How about trying to get some sleep?' she suggested. 'Things always look better in the morning.' She stood up and held out a hand to Sandie. 'Come up now, and go out with that nice young doctor if he asks you, as I'm sure he will. He's just what you need in your present state of mind.'

When Sandie was called to the telephone the next morning she was surprised to hear Anita's voice on the other end of the line.

'Hello, Sandie. I was ringing on the off-chance, really. I didn't know if you'd be home but I rather hoped you would be,' she said. 'I arrived late last night only to find that Drew wasn't at home. My own fault for not letting him know I was coming, I suppose. He still isn't here this morning, and as I have to go back to London tonight it looks as though I might not even see him. Look, as you were disappointed last time, how about coming over for a ride?'

Sandie's heart plunged. So Drew had not returned after taking Eve back to her hotel? Of course, he *had* told Tommy that he would look in at the hospital, but it was unlikely that he would have stayed all night. She remembered Tommy's remark. *'I've never seen a more determined look in a woman's eyes . . .'*

'Sandie? Are you still there?' Anita was waiting for a reply.

'Oh! Sorry, yes, I'm still here and I'd love to come over for a ride, Anita. Thank you for ringing.'

'Are you all right?' Anita sounded concerned.

'Yes, of course. I'm fine! Look, give me half an

hour and I'll be there. I'm really looking forward to it.'

She found Anita waiting for her in the stable-yard, looking tanned and fit. As they waited for Joe to saddle the horses, she told Sandie that she had just returned from a modelling assignment in Barbados.

'How exciting. My stepmother is off for her Caribbean holiday next week,' Sandie told her. 'Though now that she's renewed her friendship with Eve Paul I think she'd quite willingly postpone it if she could.'

Anita turned to her. 'Yes, I read in the papers that her small daughter was involved in an accident. So she and your stepmother are old friends, are they?'

'They were at school together. As a matter of fact she and Drew were at Elm Court last night, to dinner.'

'So that's where he was!' Joe led the horses forward and Anita mounted Fagin and headed him out through the gate, Sandie following on the little mare. For a few minutes they rode in silence, then Anita pulled her mount to one side of the lane and waited for Sandie to draw level with her.

'Did he take her home last night?' Her face was thoughtful. 'Drew, I mean.'

'Yes—but he did say he'd be looking in at the hospital afterwards.' Sandie was aware that her cheeks had coloured and she kept her head averted, but Anita was too preoccupied to notice anyway.

'I loathe her kind of woman,' she said, her brows drawn together in a frown. 'I thought it was too much to hope for—that she wouldn't try to get her hooks into him again!' She looked at Sandie. 'She hurt him pretty badly a long time ago, you know.'

'No, I didn't know,' Sandie said quietly.

They were walking the horses along the lane again and Anita looked thoughtfully at her companion as she said, 'Look, maybe I'm sticking my neck out, so tell me to mind my own business if you like, but you're pretty keen on Drew, aren't you?'

Sandie caught her breath. 'Oh dear, is it that obvious?'

Anita smiled. 'Only to someone like me.' She reached across to touch Sandie's arm. 'Don't worry, love. Your secret's safe with me. Believe me, I know how it feels. I've been through the mill myself. Last time I was home I could see that someone had really got to Drew at last. When I knew it was you I admit that I was a bit bothered at first—thought he was cradle-snatching! But then I saw how right you were for him and I changed my mind. I hope Eve isn't going to spoil things for you.'

'There's nothing to spoil. It's over,' Sandie told her bleakly. 'It was over before it started, really. Drew thinks the age-gap is too great and—and now that Eve has come back into his life—'

'But surely you're not going to sit and let her take him from you, are you?' Anita interrupted impatiently. 'Look, you might as well hear the story. I think you're entitled to be told. Years ago, when they were studying together, Drew was in love with her. Of course he was very young at the time, only a boy really, but it hit him badly. Someone else came along, you see. Someone older who could help Eve with her career, and she dropped Drew without a qualm. I was only a little girl at the time but I can still remember how miserable Drew was. I'm not going to say that it was because of Eve that he never married, but—'

'But you think it just the same,' Sandie supplied. 'I see. And now Eve is free again.'

Anita pulled a face. 'After *two* husbands. Drew would be a complete idiot if he contemplated being her third!'

'But suppose she knows now that it was Drew she loved all along?'

'If you don't mind my saying so, Sandie, I think you're being rather naive.' Anita looked at her pityingly. 'I know Eve of old and I don't think she cares tuppence about anyone's happiness but her own. I may be slightly prejudiced but I see it like this. Her singing voice isn't what it once was and she'd like to quit while she's still fairly popular. Drew has a beautiful home, a successful career and the kind of income that would keep her in the style to which she's become accustomed. She has her eye on the main chance and, as always, she's prepared to sweep all before her to get what she wants.' She looked Sandie in the eye. 'If you take my advice, you'll fight for Drew every inch of the way. He's a marvellous person and he deserves better than Eve Paul!'

Sandie looked at the glint in Anita's eyes and turned away. 'I wouldn't know how to start fighting a woman like that,' she said miserably. 'Besides, if Drew loves her there's not much I can do about it, is there?'

CHAPTER NINE

'OH! SANDIE, how long will it take to grow again?' For the first time since her operation Donna was looking at herself in a mirror. She had been moved that morning to the private wing and Sandie was unpacking her things and putting them away. She turned to look at her small patient, who was staring with dismay at her reflection in a hand mirror.

'I look like a hedgehog!' Donna wailed. She dropped the mirror on to the counterpane and looked up at Sandie, her lower lip trembling. 'Do you know, my hair had never been cut. It was ten years old, the same as me—and now it's all gone!'

Sandie put down the nightdress she had been folding and crossed the room, smiling. 'It really couldn't be helped, you know. Think how painful it would have been if your hair had stuck to the dressing. It will grow again in no time, you'll see. Don't you think it will be nice to have a change of style?'

But Donna looked no happier. 'Daddy liked it long,' she said in a small voice. 'He would have hated me this way.'

Sandie sat on the edge of the bed and took the child's hand. 'I think he would have been happy to have had you well again. I'm sure you know that,' she said gently. 'Now, cheer up. Mr Maxwell will be here to see you soon. If he sees you looking so unhappy he might think you need a new nurse.'

Donna blinked away the tears that had gathered at the corners of her eyes. 'Oh, he wouldn't really, would he?'

Sandie laughed. 'You never know! I think we'd both better be on our best behaviour, don't you?'

She had returned to Hartmoor the previous evening and settled in again at the nurses' home, feeling bleak and depressed after her talk with Anita. Jenny Sammes had been away and with no one to talk to Sandie had gone to bed early and was glad to be back at work this morning. Now, at any moment she would have to face Drew again. The prospect did nothing to cheer her.

She picked up a comb and tidied Donna's cropped hair, checking as she did so that the dressing over the operation site was firmly in place.

'Mr Maxwell will probably say that you can have your stitches out today,' she told Donna. 'Then as soon as you're properly healed you'll be able to have your hair re-styled. Tell you what, I'll find you some magazines and you can find a new short style. They're all the rage this summer.'

Donna looked up at her. 'Does Eve know it's been cut off? She hasn't seen me without my bandages yet, has she?'

'That's true. She may not have realised.'

'Oh—oh. I bet there'll be trouble when she does!' Donna pulled a face. 'She already thinks I'm a plain child, you know. This sure won't help!'

Sandie tried to hide a smile. Donna was a funny little girl with her odd mixture of innocence and precociousness. Her slight American accent and turn of phrase gave her a worldliness that belied her childish appearance.

'It's my guess that she'll enjoy helping you to choose a new style,' she said, flicking the child's hair forward into a fringe. 'Do you know, I believe it's going to curl now that it's short.' She put down the comb. 'Now, we'd better take your temperature before Mr Maxwell gets here or he'll think I'm neglecting my duty.'

She had just finished marking up Donna's chart when the door opened and Drew walked in.

'Good morning. And how's my favourite patient this morning?' He smiled and sat on the edge of the bed. 'How does it feel to be in a room of your own, eh? You're looking fine without your bandages.'

Donna grimaced. 'You've got to be kidding! I look terrible! I'll tell you one thing—you'd never get a job as a hairdresser!'

Drew laughed. 'Well, I can't take the credit for the hair-do, Donna, but it couldn't be helped. I'm sure it will soon grow again.' He stood up and looked at Sandie. 'How is she? Not upset by the move?' he asked quietly.

'No—fine.' She handed him the chart, then began to remove the dressing so that he could examine the operation site.

'Mmm.' He hung the chart back on the end of the bed and examined the sutures. 'Beginning to pull a little bit, are they, Donna? Well, I think we can ask Staff to take them out for you later today.'

Donna looked up at him anxiously. 'Will it hurt, having them taken out?'

'Only the tiniest bit for a second,' Drew assured her. 'And after that you can forget all about them.'

'And what about my legs? When will they work properly again?' she asked him. 'And why don't they now? It was my head that got hurt.'

Drew sat down again on the bed. 'You're right,' he said. 'When you had your accident your head took a very nasty knock. You don't remember much about it because you were unconscious for a while. Because of that knock the part of your brain that makes your legs work has forgotten how to do its job. It's still bruised, you see. Now, when you're a little bit better, maybe tomorrow, we shall be sending it back to school.'

Donna giggled. 'How can we do that?'

'I shall be sending a very nice lady to see you,' he told her. 'Her name is Miss Phelps and she is called a physiotherapist. She will teach you how to do some exercises to get those legs working again.'

'I see.' The large brown eyes looked up at him appealingly. 'And how long before I can go home again?'

Drew glanced at Sandie. 'Have you told her about Elm Court yet?'

She shook her head. 'I was leaving that to her stepmother.'

Donna was looking from one to the other, her head on one side like a small, bright-eyed robin. 'What is it? Do tell me!'

Drew patted her shoulder. 'All in good time, young lady. Your stepmother has a surprise for you, but she'd never forgive me if I stole her thunder and let the cat out of the bag. You'll have to wait.' He stood up. 'Behave yourself as you're doing now and you'll be out of here in no time. Bye-bye now.'

Sandie followed him into the corridor. 'She

seems to be coming along nicely. Have you any idea when you might discharge her?'

He considered for a moment, rubbing his chin thoughtfully. 'Give it another week. I'd like to see how she responds to physio.' He looked at her. 'No doubt you'll be wanting to make your own arrangements.'

She nodded. 'Well, yes.'

'I've had a word with Miss Crawford, recommending that you are released to nurse Donna.' He gave her a wry smile. 'I wasn't too popular, I might add, but in the end she agreed.'

Sandie frowned. 'It hardly seems fair. Other patients have to manage—' She broke off as she noticed his expression.

'Are you questioning my judgment?' he asked her sternly. 'I'm not just suggesting this because the child's mother happens to be a friend, you know. There's no question of special favours. Eve could easily engage a private nurse. I happen to believe that the child needs *you*, and that is what I told Miss Crawford.'

Sandie looked at the floor. 'I see. Thank you.'

'Don't thank me. I've done no more than what I consider to be right.'

She looked up at him. 'Have you any special instructions—for Donna, I mean?'

He shook his head. 'I'm a little concerned about those legs. It's not a true paralysis. I'm arranging for some tests. In the meantime I'd like her to be kept fairly quiet. I've already told Eve this, but you may find that you'll have to remind her. I think that's all.' He began to walk away and Sandie's heart sank. The formality between them this morning cut her and she longed for some note of warmth, one soft word . . .

'I hope—I hope you enjoyed Madeleine's dinner party,' she said awkwardly.

He turned. 'Very much. A very pleasant evening.'

'I went riding with Anita yesterday morning,' she told him. 'Perhaps you haven't seen her. She said you hadn't been home.' The moment she had said it she bit her tongue with embarrassment. It had slipped out without her thinking. Now he would guess at what was in her mind. He looked down at her, one eyebrow slightly raised, the grey eyes cool.

'I stayed at the flat on Saturday night. I was late—'

'Oh, please!' Sandie's cheeks were crimson. 'I didn't mean—it isn't any of my business what you did.'

'As it happens, I did go home yesterday,' he told her. 'I saw Anita just before she left and she mentioned that you'd been over to ride. I hope you enjoyed it.'

'Yes—yes, thank you.' Inside her there was an aching void. It was all over; *really* all over. Everything about him told her so; his eyes, cool as ice, his formal manner. It was almost impossible to imagine that he had held her in his arms, kissed her. It was as though the whole thing were some figment of her imagination—a fantasy. He smiled briefly and turned away, but at that moment the doors at the end of the corridor opened and Eve appeared, looking radiant in a sapphire blue suit. Her hair was arranged in a halo of gleaming blonde curls and she carried a huge sheaf of red roses. The moment she saw Drew her eyes lit up.

'Darling! I'm so glad I've caught you. Would it be possible for me to bring a photographer in this afternoon? He's from a magazine and I promise you *faithfully* that it won't take more than a minute. They're doing this article on famous stepmothers, you see and—' Her smile slowly faded as Drew shook his head.

'Oh.' The beautiful mouth pouted. 'But Donna is so much better and there are no other patients to disturb up here, surely?'

'I don't want her to have any kind of excitement at the moment,' he told her firmly. 'Wait until she's discharged and you've moved to Elm Court.'

'But that will be much too late!' Eve said petulantly. She glanced at Sandie as though she resented her presence. 'Oh well, I suppose we must do as the doctor says, mustn't we, Sandie? Oh, by the way,' she smiled at Drew again, 'thank you again for a wonderful day yesterday. It seems ages since I went out to enjoy myself. By the way, did you happen to find my scarf? I think I may have left it at the flat.'

Sandie turned away. 'I'd better get back to Donna,' she muttered, but they seemed not to have heard her.

Donna looked up as she came into the room. 'Did I hear Eve's voice?'

'Yes, and she's brought you the most gorgeous flowers,' Sandie said, forcing a smile as she tidied the bed.

'I expect she's talking to Mr Maxwell,' Donna said. 'She likes him, doesn't she—a lot?'

'They're old friends,' Sandie said evasively, stacking Donna's books neatly on the bedside locker.

'You like him too. I can tell. Oh well, I suppose he is quite good-looking, if you prefer older men.'

Sandie stared at her small patient, but before she had time to make a reply the door opened and Eve came in, thrusting the roses at her.

'Be an angel and find a vase for these.' She looked at Donna. 'Well, how's my—' She stopped short, staring in horror at the child's hair. 'Oh my God! What have they done to your lovely hair?'

Sandie saw the child's eyes fill with tears and fervently wished that Eve had more tact.

'If you take a look you'll see that it's growing in quite curly,' she put in quickly. 'I believe it will suit her beautifully, don't you?' She looked hard at Eve, who seemed to get the message.

'Oh! Oh, yes, of course. Once we get you out of here, darling, we can get it cut properly. Don't worry. We'll make a beauty of you yet.'

'I don't want to be a beauty,' Donna said sulkily.

Eve sat on the edge of the bed. 'Don't be silly, darling. All little girls want to be beautiful. Now, listen, I have a lovely surprise for you. Mr Maxwell says that you might be able to leave the hospital in about a week and I bet you can't guess where we're going?'

Donna shrugged disconsolately. 'Back to London, I guess.'

'No. We're going to the lovely house in the country where Sandie lives. Her stepmother and I are old friends and she says we can stay there until you're quite better. Won't that be nice?'

Donna looked up at her with dull eyes. 'We can't go. You know we can't. You have to rehearse for your new TV show. You told me so.'

'I was *coming* to that!' Clearly Eve's patience was wearing thin. 'Of course I wouldn't dream of leaving you there on your own, so Sandie is coming with us. It's all arranged with the hospital and everything. Now, what do you say to that?'

The child's eyes brightened again and she looked at Sandie, who was arranging the roses. 'Is it really true? Are you coming?'

Sandie nodded. 'I certainly am. So you'd better hurry up and get well, hadn't you?' She glanced at Eve. 'Would you like some coffee, Miss Paul?'

'I'd love some. And please, call me Eve. If we're going to share the same house it won't do to be formal, will it?'

'No, I suppose not.' Sandie reached for the door handle. 'I'll just go and make it for you.'

She was still in the ward kitchen, waiting for the kettle to boil, when Eve joined her.

'Is Donna really doing well?' she asked. 'She seems rather scratchy to me. I would have thought that having her own room would cheer her up.'

'The move may have tired her. She's still weak, you know,' Sandie reminded her. 'And of course, she was a little upset about her hair. It might be as well if she rested for the rest of the day.'

'Is that a polite way of telling me to get lost?' Eve looked vaguely amused.

'No, of course it isn't. You're entitled to come and go as you please,' Sandie said. 'I'm only advising you.'

Eve regarded her for a moment. 'It seems to me

that everyone around here is a little on edge this morning. Even Drew.' She looked at Sandie, one eyebrow raised. 'But I mustn't breathe a word of criticism about your hero, must I?'

'My hero?' Sandie was annoyed to feel her cheeks burning.

'It isn't surprising that you have a crush on him,' Eve said languidly. 'I dare say you're not the only nurse in this hospital who has. Doctors, especially surgeons, are romantic figures, aren't they? But one mustn't lose sight of the fact that they're still men—capable of all the same failings as other men.'

Sandie picked up the tray. 'Really? I wouldn't know. Shall we take the coffee back to Donna's room?'

Eve wrinkled her brow in exaggerated regret. 'Oh dear, I've upset you now. How clumsy of me. I'm sorry, Sandie.'

'Not at all.' Sandie pushed open the door with one foot and walked out into the corridor.

In Donna's room Eve threw herself gracefully into the chair by the window, watching Sandie shrewdly as she poured the coffee.

'What a lovely view there is up here,' she remarked. 'And I must say, it will be lovely to be able to come and go when I like without Sister Milton's laser-beam eyes boring holes into me.' She turned to Donna. 'Just think, darling, I shall be able to be with you as much as I like. You know, after I left you yesterday afternoon I was so depressed that I rang Mr Maxwell—Drew—and do you know what he did? He came right over to the hotel and fetched me and he took me out for a lovely tea. He showed me the cosy little flat where he stays when he's on call and then later we went to his lovely house in the country. It's so beautiful and peaceful there—not very far from where we'll be staying.'

Donna nodded. 'It sounds great.'

Eve looked up at Sandie as she handed her her cup. 'I understand you know Anita, Drew's sister?'

Sandie nodded. 'Yes, I do.'

Eve stirred her coffee thoughtfully. 'She mentioned that you'd been there yesterday morning to ride with her. She didn't seem at all pleased to see me. I can't think why. I haven't seen her for years, not since she was quite a little girl. I hate to say it, but she seems to have grown up a little on the arrogant side. I suppose her success has gone to her head. Perhaps that was the reason her marriage broke up too.'

Sandie moved to the door. If Eve was trying to draw her out on the subject of Anita she wasn't going to succeed. 'I'll leave you with Donna for a while then. If you'll just let me know when you're leaving.'

In the corridor she heaved a sigh of relief. Eve had certainly been at great pains to let her know that she and Drew were on good terms. Not that there was any need!

When she came off duty that evening, Sandie was unusually weary. She paused as she went through the hospital gardens. It was a beautiful evening, warm and mellow, with the sun slanting down through the trees, making leafy patterns on the lawn. The air was full of the scents of summer and she sat down for a moment on one of the benches to savour the tranquil atmosphere. But she hadn't been sitting there for more than a few seconds, her eyes closed, when a voice behind her broke her reverie.

'Peaceful, isn't it?'

She turned to see Tommy Bryant. 'It certainly is,' she agreed.

He sat down companionably beside her. 'What's up? Had a bad day?'

'No.' She shook her head. 'Quite an easy one really, specialling Donna Fenning in the private wing.'

His bright eyes searched hers. 'Someone been bugging you then? Something's wrong, I can see it is. Want to tell Uncle Tommy all about it?'

'It's nothing really—I'm just feeling a bit low.'

He slipped an arm along the back of the seat behind her. 'Just the evening for that date with me then. Suppose I pick you up in about an hour?'

Sandie opened her mouth to protest, then closed it again. She simply hadn't the energy to argue with him. Besides, she did need cheering up. She sighed. 'All right then.'

He pulled a comic face. 'Well you needn't sound so enthusiastic about it!' He grinned. 'Catch'em while their resistance is low, that's my motto. Put your posh frock on. I'm taking you somewhere special.'

She looked at him. 'Oh, where?'

'Wait and see!' He dropped a light kiss on her cheek. 'See you later then.'

When she opened the door to him an hour later he gave a long, low whistle of approval. She wore the dress she had bought for a friend's birthday party just before she had moved to the Cotswolds. It was perfectly plain and slimly cut in a silky material that flattered her slender figure. Its subtle jade green complemented her tawny hair, which she wore brushed out loosely.

'You look like some exotic wood nymph,' Tommy told her as he took her hand and hurried her down to his waiting car.

The Kingfisher was a riverside hotel deep in the heart of the country not far from Stratford-on-Avon. The restaurant was at the rear, overlooking a peaceful stretch of water. The waiter showed them to a table near the window and Sandie looked out with delight as swans sailed majestically past, gliding in and out of the willow fronds.

'What a lovely place!'

'I thought you'd like it,' Tommy said. 'It wasn't difficult to get a table, being so early in the week. They're always booked up at the weekends. This place was supposed to be a favourite haunt of Will Shakespeare's. I bet it wasn't much like this in his day though!'

Sandie looked at him. 'It must be madly expensive. You shouldn't really have brought me here, Tommy.'

For a moment he looked pensive. 'No, you're right in a way, I shouldn't. Don't tell a soul, but I'm supposed to be on duty tonight.' He held up a hand as she opened her mouth to protest. 'It's all right, they know where I am and I've had a word with the head waiter. He'll let me know immediately if they get a call.'

Sandie was shocked. 'But there was no need! Any night would have done.'

He covered her hand with his. 'Ah, but who could have resisted you, sitting there so pale and wan among the flowers?'

A waiter came and took their order. In one corner of the room a group of musicians played and Tommy stood up and held out his hand.

'Dance while we're waiting?'

More diners began to arrive as they circled the floor and Sandie looked around her with interest. 'I'm sure this must be very popular,' she said. Tommy nodded.

'There aren't many places that have its unique atmosphere—' She heard him draw in his breath sharply. 'Oh my God! That's torn it!' He stopped dancing. 'Look, do you mind if we sit down now?'

Sandie looked at him. 'What is it? Is something wrong?'

He smiled ruefully. 'You could say that.'

She followed his eyes and the next moment her heart almost stopped. A group of people had just come into the restaurant. They followed a waiter to a table on the other side of the room. There were two couples—and one of them was Eve, escorted by Drew. Sandie's heart skipped a beat as she looked at Tommy.

'Do you want to leave?'

'Not likely, when we've ordered our dinner,' he said defiantly.

They sat down and began to eat the food that was brought to them, but for Sandie at least the evening was quite spoilt. If Drew saw them he would blame her for Tommy's absence, and as the moments ticked by it seemed more and more inevitable that they would be seen.

They managed to get as far as the sweet before it happened. It was Eve who spotted them. Out of the corner of her watchful eye, Sandie saw her lean forward to tap Drew on the arm and nod in their direction. A moment later he was on his way across the room to them, a purposeful gleam in his eye. Tommy muttered under his breath, 'Oh well, here it comes!'

'Good evening.' Drew seemed to tower over them, his eyes glinting coldly as he looked down at them. 'Correct me if I'm wrong, but aren't you supposed to be on duty tonight, Bryant?'

Tommy cleared his throat. 'Well, strictly speaking, yes. I've left word where I am, of course.'

'I think you know my views on this kind of thing,' Drew said, his voice dangerously low and controlled. 'I made an exception on Saturday but I didn't expect you to take advantage of it. The twenty minutes it would take you to get back to Hartmoor could mean life or death for someone, and you know it!' He flashed a glance at Sandie before he said, 'If you've finished your meal I suggest that you get back to the hospital immediately.'

Tommy looked across at Sandie, his face a dull red. 'When Sandie has finished,' he began. Drew stopped him with a look.

'No—now! When Staff Nurse Masters has finished her meal I will see that she gets back safely. You need have no worries on that score!'

For a moment Tommy looked as though he was about to argue, then he thought better of it and reluctantly stood up, looking apologetically at Sandie.

'I'll settle the bill on my way out,' he told her. 'Sorry about this. See you later.'

When he had gone, Sandie looked up at Drew, her eyes flashing angrily. 'Was there any need to be quite so vicious with him?' She knew she was being impertinent. For a mere staff nurse to speak to a consultant in this way was madness, but at that moment she couldn't have cared less. He ignored her question.

'Have you finished or are you going to have coffee?'

She pushed her half-eaten sweet to one side. 'Do you really expect me to sit here calmly and eat the rest of my meal after that?' She stood up. 'And you needn't trouble yourself to see me home. I'd far rather go by myself.'

His hand closed firmly round her upper arm. 'I said I'd take you and I will,' he said between clenched teeth. 'Kindly do not make a scene.'

She glared at him. 'I don't think I need *you* to tell me that!'

As they passed the table where Eve and the other couple sat, Drew paused. Eve looked up at them enquiringly.

'Is anything wrong?'

'Dr Bryant has been called back to the hospital,' Drew told her. 'Sandie has no way of getting back to Hartmoor so I'm going to take her. I shan't be long, but please don't wait for me.'

'But why doesn't Sandie join us?' Eve invited. 'Then we can drop her off on our way back and you won't have to make a special journey.'

But before Sandie could reply Drew said, 'She has to get back now. I'll return as soon as I can.'

Pushing her in front of him, he made his way to the door, still clutching her arm in an iron grip. When they reached it she turned, her face pink with anger.

'Do you mind if I collect my coat from the cloakroom? You can stand at the window if you like, to see that I don't escape!'

'I'll be waiting for you in the front entrance,' he said shortly, ignoring her sarcasm. 'And please don't be all night about it.'

She collected her velvet jacket from the cloakroom and joined him in the entrance hall where he was walking up and down like a caged lion. Without a word he took her arm again and hurried her out to the car park, walking so quickly that she was forced to run to keep up with him.

'Do—you mind?' she asked breathlessly. 'You're hurting my arm!'

He stopped, letting her go as he took the car keys from his pocket and unlocked the passenger door. 'I'm sorry. Get in,' he ordered brusquely.

She waited for him to get into the car, then turned to him, her heart beating fast. 'You have absolutely no right to treat me like this,' she said, her voice shaking. 'I'm off duty and there is no reason why I shouldn't go wherever I please!'

He switched on the ignition, his mouth a thin, tight line. 'You have no business to encourage my registrar away from his duties. That is quite unforgivable.'

'*Oh!*' It was almost a wail. 'I didn't! I had no idea he was supposed to be on duty. He simply asked me out for dinner and I said yes.'

Drew edged the car on to the road, keeping his

eyes straight ahead. 'You have been at Hartmoor General for long enough now to know that Dr Bryant has a weakness for nurses,' he said stiffly. 'That's all right as long as he doesn't allow it to interfere with his work. Tonight he has, and I won't tolerate it.' He shot her a searing glance. 'I must say that I thought you had a more adult attitude towards your work. I'm disappointed in you.'

Sandie caught her breath. He could hardly have made a more stinging comment, striking at her age *and* her dedication to her work. 'I seem to remember you congratulating me on what you described as my "choice" only the other day,' she retorted. 'You told me that Tommy Bryant was just what I needed—which is *more* proof that you don't really know me at all. I—I—' She was unable to go on, her throat almost closing with angry tears. Drew drove on, seemingly unruffled.

'It might be better if we dropped the subject,' he said at last. 'When I said that, I didn't mean you to make a fool of yourself. It seems I was wrong. Bryant seems to bring out the worst in you.'

The threatening tears suddenly turned to red-hot fury as she turned to glare at him, eyes flashing.

'You talk about *me* making a fool of myself!' she flung at him. 'Don't you realise it's you who is the laughing-stock of the hospital? The way you bow and scrape to Eve Paul! Everyone knows she has you completely under her thumb and that it's only a matter of t—' She trailed off as he braked suddenly, swerving the car into the side of the road and bringing it to a halt. One look at his face was enough to tell her that she had disturbed his control. He was angry, really angry. He switched of the ignition and turned to her, his eyes glittering with cold fury.

'Would you kindly explain your last remark?'

She moistened her dry lips, determined not to climb down. 'I—well, it's true. Everyone is saying she has you where she wants you. *Hooked* was the word I heard used, if you really want to know!'

'I see. And would you mind telling me who the mysterious "they" are?'

'It's the general opinion!' She thrust out her chin defiantly.

'Including yours?'

Her eyes jerked away from his. 'What else am I to think?'

'You are not paid to think or to have opinions about me or any of the other doctors in the hospital,' he told her coldly. 'You are paid to nurse and I suggest that you concentrate all your energy on that in future. Lately you seem keener on making an exhibition of yourself in corridors with irresponsible young registrars!' He switched on the ignition again and nosed the car back on to the road, his eyes looking straight ahead. 'It's lucky it was only I who saw you that night. If it had been your SNO you would have been in trouble.'

Sandie's heart was beating fast as she stared at his profile. 'I see. Thank you very much. I'm *most* grateful.'

He did not return her look. 'That's quite all right. Just see that it doesn't happen again.'

The rest of the journey was spent in a silence so charged with electricity that it almost crackled. As Drew halted the car outside the rear entrance to the nurses' home he turned to her.

'If you can tear your thoughts away from Bryant, and from the private lives of the senior members of the hospital staff, there is something I'd like you to do for me,' he said. When she didn't reply he went on. 'I'm concerned about Donna Fenning's lack of mobility. I'm sure that the tests will show that there is no reason for it—no physical reason, that is. I'd like you to try to find out if anything is troubling her. Will you do that?'

She reached for the door handle. 'Of course I will.' She turned to look at him, biting her lip. 'It isn't true, what you said about my being preoccupied with the private lives of others. I'm not a busybody. As for Tommy Bryant—'

'Please!' He held up a hand, stopping her in mid-sentence. 'Spare me the details. If you don't mind, I think I've heard enough on the subject for one evening.' He leaned across and opened the door for her. 'Goodnight.' He revved the engine impatiently as she got out.

Sandie slammed the door and ran in through the nurses' home entrance, keeping her head averted so that he wouldn't see the scalding tears that poured down her cheeks.

CHAPTER TEN

THE REST of the week was busier than Sandie had expected. Sally Phelps, the physiotherapist, came each morning to put Donna through her routine of exercises, but she confessed privately to Sandie that the child's legs seemed to be making no progress at all. It was arranged that the treatment should continue after Donna had moved to Elm Court.

Sandie saw Drew only briefly. He told her that Donna's tests had proved negative. There was no reason why she should not make a full recovery. At the weekend he decided to discharge her from hospital, hoping that the more relaxed atmosphere at Elm Court would be beneficial. Sandie moved with her patient on Saturday afternoon and on Monday morning Eve departed for London to begin her rehearsals, while Madeleine was busy preparing for her holiday. No one had mentioned the incident at The Kingfisher and Sandie thought she had heard the last of it until one evening, when Eve managed to get away from her rehearsals early and drove to Upper Longden for an overnight stay. When Donna had been put to bed she quizzed Sandie about it, bringing up the subject as they were having coffee after dinner.

'What a pity your evening out with young Dr Bryant was spoilt. You must have felt very annoyed with Drew.' She was watching Sandie with narrowed eyes. 'I can't think why he found it so necessary to take you home immediately though, unless of course you asked him to.'

Sandie shrugged, determined not to be drawn by Eve's probing. 'I certainly didn't do that,' she said calmly.

'You could have joined us as I suggested,' Eve went on. 'The couple we were with were cousins of mine—with whom I hope to go into business. The people Donna and I were visiting when the accident happened. The evening out was their idea. It was meant as a kind of thank-you to Drew for all he has done, so it really looked rather bad, his running off like that.' Her eyes swept over Sandie speculatively. 'Especially as he was gone for so long. It was very awkward for me.'

Sandie began to put the coffee cups on to the tray. 'It's at least twenty minutes each way between Hartmoor and The Kingfisher,' she remarked.

'Exactly—and Drew was gone for over an hour!'

Sandie straightened up and looked at her. 'Perhaps the traffic was heavy.'

Eve's eyes flashed dangerously but she chose to ignore the remark. 'Sandie, while we're alone like this I'd like to take the opportunity to have a little talk with you. I hope you won't mind if I speak frankly?'

'Of course not.' Sandie sat down.

Eve smiled. 'I realise that Drew is attractive. I'm sure there are a good many hearts fluttering for him at Hartmoor, but I think someone should tell you that your attempts at catching his attention are ludicrously transparent. I'm telling you this for your own good because I hate to see anyone making a fool of themselves.'

Sandie flushed. 'I think you're mistaken.'

'I hope I am, but I don't think so. You see, Sandie, I know Drew very well—well enough to know that you shouldn't read too much into his kindness. He's very single-minded and I happen to know where his future plans lie.'

Sandie caught her breath but she tried not to let Eve see her disquiet. 'I don't quite see why you're telling me this,' she said.

'I simply wanted to put you straight,' Eve said. 'That's only fair. Underneath all that skill and dedication, Drew is still a man and I'm sure you wouldn't want to spoil his career for the sake of a whim.'

Sandie frowned. 'A whim?'

'It's a kind of status thing with young nurses, isn't it? It's fun to see how many doctors one can date. Do you have a points system? Consultants must rate high!'

Sandie got to her feet. 'I find that remark very offensive,' she said. 'Perhaps under the circumstances it might be better if I asked to be taken off Donna's case.'

'No! Don't do that.' Eve jumped to her feet. 'I was only trying to advise you for your own good, Sandie—as an older woman. That was a stupid remark. I apologise. I'd really like us to be friends and I'm sure we can be. Donna adores you. It would set her recovery back if you left her now and I know you wouldn't want that.'

Sandie glanced at her watch. 'I'd better go up and check Donna,' she muttered. 'Perhaps we can talk some other time.'

Eve held out her hand. 'Of course. I want you to know that I'm only concerned with Drew's happiness. I owe him such a lot. Donna's illness has brought us very close together again.'

Outside in the hall Sandie stood for a moment, drawing a deep breath and trying to collect herself. The scene with Eve had been embarrassing and uncomfortable. Clearly she meant to keep Drew to herself, now that she had found him again. Tommy had been right about that. As she went up the stairs, Sandie wished she hadn't grown so fond of Donna. She would have given anything to be taken off the case—to be as far from Eve Paul as possible. As it was, she felt committed. What did Drew intend to do about Eve, she wondered? He hadn't denied the rumours she had thrown at him the other night.

Eve left after breakfast the following morning and for the rest of the day Donna was quiet. The child seemed tired and Sandie began to wonder if the physiotherapy sessions were proving too much for her. She didn't press her when she refused her lunch but when she pushed away the dish of ice-cream at tea-time Sandie grew really concerned. Donna's little face was pale and there were dark shadows under her eyes. Taking her pulse and temperature, Sandie found that they were normal. She must look for the cause elsewhere.

'Is your head hurting?' She laid a cool hand on the child's forehead. 'You've been so quiet since Eve left this morning.'

The large brown eyes looked up at her. 'She still wants me to go to that dumb school. She's started talking about it all over again.'

Sandie smiled. 'School! Is that all? Tell me, what dumb school is it?'

Donna sighed. 'It's this stage school. I don't want to go. I told her so before. I'll hate it!' A large tear began to trickle down her cheek and Sandie silently cursed Eve for her timing in bringing the matter up again. She sat down and took the child's hand.

'Now, now, I'm sure it can't be as bad as that. You'll probably love every minute of it when you're quite better and feeling more like school again.'

'But I want to go back to my old school,' Donna wailed. 'I don't want to be an actress, so why should I go to a stage school? I'm terrible at singing and dancing and all those things. I *know* what I want to be when I grow up!'

'And what's that?' Sandie asked gently.

'A nurse.'

Sandie smiled. 'Well, that's good. But are you sure it isn't just being in hospital that makes you want that? Lots of people go out wanting to be doctors and nurses you know. Usually it wears off.'

But Donna shook her head. 'I wanted to be a nurse before my accident. Eve just won't listen. Sandie—she can't *make* me go, can she? I mean, she isn't my real mother.'

'No, but she is your guardian—the person responsible for you and for your education,' Sandie explained. 'I expect she just wants you to have the widest possible choice. You know, that's the best part of being a child. There's so much time in which to make up your mind.'

Donna sighed. 'But you should just see that place! All those kids who think they're going to be big-shot actors! I don't see how I'd bear it. I'd run away.' She looked at Sandie from under the thick, dark lashes. 'There is one thing. If my legs never get to work properly again I won't be able to go, will I?'

Sandie drew the tray towards her again. 'I don't think we'll talk about that. Now, I'm sure you can eat this ice-cream before it melts, can't you?'

But Donna shook her head, her eyes filling with tears again. 'Why doesn't Grannie Fenning write or come to see me?' she asked. 'Do you think she knows about my accident?'

Sandie frowned. It was the first time she had heard any mention of a grandmother. 'Where does she live, Donna?' she asked gently. 'Is she in America?'

The child nodded unhappily. 'Yes. I used to see her twice a year until Daddy died. Then she wanted me to go back there to live, but Eve wanted me to stay with her. She promised me we'd have a house in the country—that I could have a pony and riding lessons, all that stuff. So I wrote and told Grannie I wanted to stay here.'

Sandie squeezed her hand. 'I'm sure she understood.'

'She didn't write to me any more. I guess she must have been angry with me. I miss her, Sandie.' Donna sniffed hard as the tears spilled over. 'She wouldn't make me go to a school I didn't want, I know she wouldn't.'

Sandie put her arms round the sobbing child. 'Now, Donna, you mustn't upset yourself like this. I'm sure there's a misunderstanding. If Eve knew you hated the idea of the school this much I'm sure she wouldn't insist on you going there.'

'She would! That day—the day I had the accident—we'd been arguing about it. I got mad and took the bike and rode off. It was too big for me to manage properly and—well you know—'

Sandie managed to get Donna to settle down for a rest in her room and when she was asleep she went down to the hall and dialled Drew's office. His secretary told her he was busy and asked if she would like to speak to Dr Bryant.

'No, but if you could leave Mr Maxwell a message to ring me here at Elm Court as soon as he can, I'd be grateful,' Sandie said. 'It's quite important—concerning his patient, Donna Fenning.'

As she replaced the receiver Madeleine came down the stairs carrying two large cases.

'Well, I'm ready. All I have to do now is to wait for the taxi,' she said. 'We sail tomorrow morning at seven. What an unearthly hour!' She broke off as she noticed Sandie's worried expression. 'Is anything wrong, dear? Here I am rambling on about my holiday—is it Donna?'

Sandie nodded. 'I'm a little concerned about her. She seems low and her legs aren't getting any stronger. I've a hunch I know why, but if anything it only makes the problem worse!'

Madeleine shook her head sympathetically. 'Oh dear. Look, I haven't much time, but if there's anything I can do?'

'There might be.' Sandie looked at her. 'Have you got a few minutes to talk, Maddie, before you go?'

'Of course, the taxi isn't due for half an hour.' Madeleine pushed open the door of the drawing-room. 'Come in here and sit down. We might as well be comfortable.'

When they were seated Sandie looked at her stepmother. 'Has Eve ever mentioned Donna's grandmother to you? Or spoken of some school she's determined to send Donna to?'

Madeleine looked uncomfortable. 'Well, yes. She did say something—but it was in confidence.'

'Nevertheless, I think you should tell me,' Sandie said firmly. 'Donna was extremely upset after Eve left this morning. She mentioned her grandmother, too. I didn't even know there was a grandmother. Has Eve notified her of Donna's accident?'

'I've no idea whether she has or not,' Madeleine told her. 'It seems she wanted the child to go and live with her in America but Eve wouldn't— *couldn't* allow it. You see, her husband had left money to be used for Donna's education and Eve has invested it all in a stage school that she and her cousin are running. To justify the investment Donna has to attend the school, but for some reason she didn't want her mother-in-law to know anything about all this.'

'I don't suppose she did!' Light dawned. Suddenly everything fell neatly into place and Sandie saw the reason for Eve's behaviour. Carefully she explained to her stepmother what had happened. Madeleine looked worried.

'Oh dear. I'm beginning to regret offering her the use of the house now. I have an awful feeling that there are going to be complications and you are going to land right in the middle of them!' She shook her head. 'If only I wasn't going to be away!'

Sandie touched her arm reassuringly. 'Don't worry. I was telephoning Drew when you came downstairs. He was busy, but I left a message for him to ring me as soon as he could. I'm sure he'll know what to do.'

Madeleine looked relieved. 'Oh, I'm sure he will. If anyone can handle Eve he will be able to.' She looked up sharply at Sandie. 'Oh, I'm sorry, darling, what a thoughtless thing to say.' She reached out to touch Sandie's hand. 'Does it still hurt?'

Sandie shook her head. 'My only fear is that he'll think I'm trying to blacken Eve's character.' She didn't tell her stepmother about the violent quarrel they had had or the things she had said.

It was several hours before he rang her back. Maddie had been waved off in her taxi; they had finished dinner and Donna had been in bed and asleep for almost an hour. Sitting alone in the drawing-room the telephone's ring startled her. When he spoke his voice sounded tense.

'Hallo, you wanted me to ring? I've only just come into the office and found your message on tape. What's the trouble?'

'I wanted to have a word with you about Donna,' Sandie told him. 'You remember you asked me to try to find out of anything was troubling her?'

'I do—and you think there is?'

'Yes, but you must be tired. It can wait until tomorrow.'

'No, it can't. I'm going away first thing in the morning.' There was a pause, then he asked, 'Is there anyone there besides you? Anyone you could leave with Donna?'

'Well, yes. Mrs Simmons is here. She's living in while Maddie's away, to help me, but—'

'Can you borrow your stepmother's car and drive

over to Hartmoor?' he asked brusquely. 'I've been operating so I'm staying at the flat tonight. I'd like to hear what you have to say before I leave.'

'How long will you be away? Maybe it could wait—'

He cut in sharply on her, 'Look, Sandie, just come, will you?'

'Of course. I'll be there in about half an hour.' As she put down the telephone she wondered if he would be so anxious to hear what she had to say once he knew what it was. As she got ready she felt apprehension stirring in the pit of her stomach. She wasn't looking forward to the coming interview one little bit.

Mrs Simmons agreed readily to keep an eye on Donna, and Sandie soon found herself driving Maddie's small saloon out through the gates of Elm Court and heading in the direction of Hartmoor. She drove the car into the car park at the rear of the block of flats and made her way towards the lift, her heart beginning to beat uncomfortably fast. Drew had been so angry on the night of their quarrel. Was he still furious with her? Would he even listen when she put her theory to him?

When he opened the door to her he looked relaxed. He wore casual slacks and a sweater and he was playing records; she could hear the strains of the Mendelssohn violin concerto drifting out from the living-room. He smiled and invited her in.

'Take your coat off.' He took it from her and hung it in the hall cupboard. 'Perhaps you'd like a drink? I was just going to have one.'

She shook her head, her mouth dry. 'I think I'd

better just say what I came to say and get back to Donna.'

He frowned. 'Are you worried about her? Do you want me to have a look at her?'

'Oh no.' She shook her head. She was handling it badly. 'I do feel responsible though. It isn't fair to leave Mrs Simmons in charge for too long.'

He put a hand under her elbow. 'Relax, Sandie. The child is in no danger. Her only problem now is the weakness in her legs and I take it that's what you're here to discuss.' He smiled. 'Please, sit down. You're making me quite nervous.'

Sandie managed to smile back and sat down reluctantly on the edge of the settee. Drew looked down ruefully at her.

'Oh dear. I think you'd better have that drink after all, don't you?'

'I'm driving.'

'I don't think one small brandy would send you over the limit,' he told her. 'Unless of course you've already had some!'

'Of course I haven't!' Sandie's eyes flashed indignantly at him until she saw that he was teasing her. There was a glint of amusement in the grey eyes. He was a very different Drew from the one who had rebuffed her so fiercely the other evening. Her cheeks coloured. 'I never drink on duty.' She bit her lip and looked away, feeling foolish.

He poured her a small measure of brandy and handed her the glass, sitting down beside her on the settee. 'I told you I was going away first thing in the morning,' he said. 'I have to go to Derbyshire for a medical conference.' He looked at her. 'I wanted to see you anyway, to get something out of the way.

I'm sorry about the other night. I was very hard on you.'

She shook her head. 'It doesn't matter.'

'Oh, but it does. Bryant told me next morning what happened. He admitted the blame was entirely his.'

She couldn't look at him. 'It's over and forgotten.' She stole a sideways look at him. 'I'm afraid that when you hear what I have to say you're going to be even angrier than you were then, so please may I get it over with?'

'Oh dear. Perhaps you'd better in that case.'

She licked her lips. 'Well, it seems that Eve has been pressuring Donna to go to a stage school in which she has some kind of financial interest.' She glanced at him. 'Perhaps you know about it.'

'Yes. She's going into partnership with a cousin, the one we were dining with that evening at The Kingfisher.'

Sandie swallowed. 'Perhaps you didn't know that she invested the money her husband left for his daughter's education in the school,' she told him. 'To justify that, it is necessary for Donna to attend the school. But the child doesn't want to go. She's making herself quite ill at the prospect. She even hinted that if her legs didn't get better she wouldn't be able to go. I honestly believe that is what is holding up her recovery.'

Drew's face clouded. He got up and walked to the window, looking thoughtfully out. He had his back towards Sandie and she couldn't tell whether he was angry or not. She cleared her throat.

'I'm sorry to have to tell you this, but you did ask.' She paused. 'There's something else.'

When she didn't go on he turned to look at her, his eyes enigmatic. 'Yes—something else?'

'Donna has a grandmother in America. Her father's mother. When he died she wanted Donna to go to her, but Eve couldn't let her go because she'd already agreed to invest the money. Donna misses her grandmother. She's fretting because she hasn't heard from her.'

Drew looked at her for a long moment. 'I see. That explains a lot. But why did you think these disclosures would make me angry?'

She looked away. 'Surely it's obvious? It is the truth, though, and I'm only telling you because you asked me to find out what was troubling Donna.'

He crossed the room again and sat beside her. 'The things you said the other night, the rumours—am I to take it that you believe them, then?'

She bit her lip. 'It isn't any of my business.'

'Do you?' He grasped her shoulders and turned her towards him.

She nodded unhappily. 'I suppose I do. What else could I believe?'

'You're right!' He let her go. 'You were supposed to believe them. When Eve suddenly reappeared, two things happened. One was that I realised there was almost a generation between you and me, and the second was that here was the perfect way to prove that to you.' He sighed. 'I also felt a certain obligation to Eve, and when she seemed so anxious about Donna I naturally wanted to do what I could to help. I didn't realise I was about to open such a Pandora's box!'

She looked up at him. 'You felt an obligation to Eve? Why?'

He smiled wryly. 'Eve doesn't know it, but because of her I made the most important decision of my life—to give up music and study medicine. You see, when we were at college we spent a lot of time together. For a while I thought I meant something to her. Then she showed me how superficial she was—how superficial and self-seeking a musical career could be, dedicated to the art itself at the expense of people. Once I recovered from the hurt of being dropped I saw that quite clearly and I never looked back. So you see, I have quite a lot to thank Eve for.'

Sandie's heart gave a great leap. 'So you're not—not in love with her?' she whispered.

He smiled. 'I may have thought I was a long time ago. I was too young then to know what being in love really meant.' His eyes darkened. 'That's why I was so shocked when you told me about the rumours that were circulating.'

For a long moment they stood looking at each other and Sandie hardly dared to breathe for fear of breaking the tension between them. At last she reached out impulsively to touch his face. Immediately he caught the hand that lay against his cheek and pressed his lips into the palm. Slowly, he drew her towards him, one arm about her waist. She felt the slight roughness of his beard as she rubbed her cheek against his. Her lips lingered at the corner of his mouth and then he was kissing her—hungrily, as though he couldn't help himself. As his arms tightened around her she could feel the quickened beating of his heart as, eyes closed, his lips explored her eyelids, her throat and then returned to her mouth, parting her lips with a hungry need that took her by storm. She clung to him, wondering how to say all the things she longed to tell him, aching to hear him say that he loved her. She looked up into his eyes.

'Drew,' she whispered. 'Drew, do you want me?'

She felt him tense in her arms. Then, drawing a deep breath, he held her at arm's length. 'Sandie, we have to talk. I want to tell you—' His words were rudely interrupted by the sudden shrilling of the telephone. For a moment he stood motionless, looking down at her. Then he dropped his hands to his sides and crossed the room to answer it.

'Maxwell here.' There was a pause, then he turned to look at her. 'It's for you.'

'For me?' She was puzzled. The only person who knew where she had gone was Mrs Simmons. It had to be something to do with Donna. She took the receiver from his outstretched hand apprehensively.

'Hallo? Mrs Simmons?'

The woman's voice sounded anxious. 'Oh, Miss Masters, thank goodness I've managed to reach you! A lady arrived here a few minutes ago, an American lady. She says her name is Mrs Fenning and that she's Donna's grandmother. She says she's come to take her home!'

CHAPTER ELEVEN

SANDIE left the flat at once to drive back to Elm Court. Drew had offered to go with her but she had assured him that she could handle the situation. He might be needed at the hospital; he also had to be up early to drive to Derbyshire.

All the way back to Upper Longden her thoughts were torn in two directions. At last Drew had indicated that he loved and wanted her and that should have made her happy, yet she couldn't help feeling apprehensive. He was to be away for a week and so much could happen. Would he have second thoughts? If only the telephone hadn't rung—if only she could have proved to him once and for all that their love was right. And this new development. What would happen now that Donna's grandmother had arrived? What would the child's reaction be? Would it upset her? Worst of all, how would Eve take it? Sandie imagined the two warring women with a sinking heart, wondering how she would cope with the situation.

When she met Mona Fenning she was slightly reassured. She was a small, slim woman, looking at least ten years younger than her sixty-five years. The moment Sandie looked into the bright brown eyes that were so like Donna's, and felt the firm handshake, she knew that the fragile look concealed an iron will. Eve would meet more than her match here, she was sure.

Mrs Simmons hovered anxiously in the background. 'I hope I did the right thing in ringing you?'

'Yes, of course. Has Donna been all right?'

'Fine. She's still fast asleep, hasn't woken since you left.'

Sandie looked at the newcomer. 'Have you had anything to eat, Mrs Fenning? May we get you something?'

Mona shook her head. 'I dined on the train, thank you, and your housekeeper has already made coffee for me.'

Her voice was soft, with a stronger version of Donna's accent. Sandie smiled apologetically.

'You must be longing to see Donna, but I'm afraid I shall have to ask you to wait until morning.'

Mona smiled. 'But of course. I wouldn't dream of asking you to wake her.' She glanced towards Mrs Simmons who was still hovering in the doorway. 'If we might talk though.' She smiled at Sandie as they sat down. 'I recognised you the moment I saw you. You're the nurse the papers called the Hartmoor Angel. I knew the minute I saw that picture that Donna would be well looked after. I've always prided myself on being a good judge of faces.'

Sandie frowned. 'You saw that picture? But how?'

The older woman smiled. 'Since my son died I've lost touch with Donna. She said she wanted to stay in England and although I wrote to her she never replied. That grieved me, although I have my own ideas about it. We used to have such a fine relationship, you see. I couldn't believe we weren't being kept apart for some reason.' She smiled. 'I have a friend in London and I asked him to try to keep me in touch. Whenever he could, he would send me magazine and newspaper articles about Eve, so that I knew where Donna was and what she was doing. You can imagine what a shock it was for me when I received the one about the accident! To hear like that, not even to have been informed! The moment I heard, I caught the first flight and when I rang the hospital at Hartmoor and explained who I was they gave me this address.'

'I'm very sorry you weren't informed, Mrs Fenning,' Sandie told her. 'I only learned about you recently. Donna misses you a great deal and I have a feeling that seeing you again will help her recovery very much.'

A determined look came into Mona's eyes. 'I intend to do more than just see her, my dear. I intend to take her home with me just as soon as it can be arranged. That is if she wants to come, of course.'

Privately Sandie thought that Donna would jump at the chance, but she kept her thoughts to herself. She stood up. 'You must be tired, Mrs Fenning. I'm sure that Mrs Simmons will have your room ready by now. If there is anything you need, please ask. In the morning I expect you'd like to telephone your daughter-in-law.'

Mona's eyes glinted determinedly. 'I've already done that! I asked your housekeeper for the number and rang her while I was waiting for you.'

Sandie paused, catching her breath. Mona Fenning certainly didn't let the grass grow under her feet. She wondered what Eve's reaction had been on hearing her mother-in-law's voice after so long. As though she read her thoughts, Mona smiled.

'I believe it came as quite a shock to her. She couldn't believe I was actually speaking from this house!'

'I dare say! Are we to expect—will she be coming here to see you?'

'You better believe she will!' Mona told her triumphantly. 'She said she'd be here just as soon as she could.'

Sandie frowned. 'I don't quite know how to say this, Mrs Fenning, but I *am* Donna's nurse, and as such I feel a certain responsibility for her. If there is to be any kind of dispute between you and Miss Paul, I'd rather Donna were kept out of it. She has had a severe head injury and although she has made a good recovery anything traumatic could set her back.'

Mona Fenning's face was concerned. 'But of course, my dear. My only thoughts are for her. I shall protect her as much as I can. Tell me, has she completely recovered or are there any after-effects from her accident?'

'One,' Sandie told her. 'There is still a slight paralysis in her legs—a persistent weakness. She has been having physiotherapy but it looks as though it could take some time.' She paused. 'To tell you the truth, I have been wondering if her lack of response to the treatment was entirely physical. It will be interesting to see what your arrival will do.'

Mona smiled. 'Oh, I just can't wait to see her in the morning.'

*   *   *

Sandie woke early next morning. For a long moment she lay sleepily watching the patterns of leafy early morning light dancing on the ceiling, collecting her thoughts and piecing them together. The events of the previous day had been surprising, to say the least. Foremost in her mind were thoughts of Drew. She hugged to herself the memory of his touch. What would have happened, she wondered, if only the telephone hadn't rung at that particular moment? Just for once, she thought wistfully of people whose careers and private lives could be kept in neat, separate compartments—jobs that could be left behind in an office at five o'clock each evening.

She closed her eyes again, fantasising about how wonderful it would have been to have wakened in Drew's arms this morning—to have cooked breakfast for him and seen him off on his trip to Derbyshire, happy in the certain knowledge that he would return to her. She thought of the elderly woman asleep in the room across the landing— Donna's grandmother. In a short time now they would be reunited. Eve would return from London and the battle would begin. A tug-o-war with the child as prize. Sandie's heart sank at the prospect and she wished fervently that Drew could be here to help and advise her. Although she was responsible for the child's well-being, she could offer only so much protection. At last, unable to rest any more, she got up, showered and dressed and tiptoed along the landing to Donna's room. As she drew back the curtains she saw Donna stir and open her eyes.

'Hi!'

'Good morning. Did you sleep well?'

'Yes. I had a funny dream though. I dreamed I was awake and I could hear Grannie Fenning's voice downstairs. I expect it was because I was talking about her yesterday.'

Sandie sat on the edge of the bed. 'Are you feeling strong? Do you think you could take a surprise—a big one?'

Donna's eyes lit up. 'A surprise? What is it? Oh, do tell, Sandie!'

'You'll see—all in good time. First I want you to eat a big breakfast. I'm going downstairs to get it now. Do you promise?'

'OK, I promise.'

Obediently Donna ate all her breakfast, then Sandie helped her to bathe and dress. Downstairs she found Mona waiting nervously.

'She's ready, you can come up now,' Sandie smiled. The older woman stood up, her hand anxiously grasping the back of her chair.

'Oh dear. Now that the moment has come I feel quite nervous. You are sure it's all right?'

Sandie nodded. 'I have an idea you might be quite the best medicine she could have!'

She had placed Donna in a chair facing the door. Outside on the landing she paused, glancing at Mona. 'She looks a little different. Her hair had to be cut short for the operation. She was rather upset about it.'

Mona nodded. 'I understand.'

Quietly, Sandie opened the door. 'Donna, here is the surprise I told you about!' She stood aside and held her breath. For a moment Donna stared incredulously at her grandmother, then she gave a little cry and rose to her feet.

'Grannie! How did you get here? How did you know where I was?'

Mona made to go to her but Sandie put out a hand to stop her. She had seen Donna take an involuntary step forward. It was followed by another, and another until, almost without knowing it, Donna had crossed half the space between them. Unable to bear the suspense another moment, Mona ran forward to catch her granddaughter in her arms.

'Oh, my baby! It's so wonderful to see you. They say you couldn't walk but you did—*you just did!*'

Sandie withdrew quietly. What she had just seen had confirmed for her what she had guessed for some time. The weakness in Donna's legs was really an unconscious protest. From now on she would go from strength to strength, as long as everything went the right way.

She began to go downstairs but she had scarcely reached the bottom when the front door opened and Eve stood on the threshold. For a moment they stared at each other, then Eve demanded,

'Where is she? Where is that woman?' Slamming the door behind her she made to push past Sandie.

'Please, don't go up.' Sandie stood her ground, barring the way. 'Donna is with her grandmother and I won't have her upset. Will you wait in the drawing-room? I'll tell her you're here.'

Eve's face was flushed and her eyes blazed at Sandie. 'I've been up since dawn. I've broken all the rules to get here, cancelled my rehearsals for the day, rearranged appointments and now you calmly tell me to *wait*!'

'I'm not telling, I'm asking—for Donna's sake. She's been very ill, remember.'

Just for a moment Sandie thought Eve was going to push her out of the way and insist on going upstairs, but then, to her relief, she turned and walked into the drawing-room. Sandie followed and closed the door.

'None of this is my business,' she said quietly. 'It must be resolved between you and Mrs Fenning. All that I ask is that Donna is kept out of any argument.'

Eve looked her up and down, a little taken aback at the calm determination and her own response to it. 'If you're so concerned for her I'm surprised that you allowed her grandmother to walk in on her,' she said. 'Just what do you imagine *that* shock will do to her?'

'It seems to have brought back the use of her legs,' Sandie told her coolly. 'She walked again this morning for the first time since her accident!'

Eve and Mona Fenning were closetted together for the rest of the morning and Sandie found it hard to keep to her normal routine. Donna was impatient and curious to know what was going on. After lunch Sally Phelps arrived and was astonished at the improvement in her patient's mobility, but she insisted that the exercises be kept up and suggested that Donna might come into the hospital daily and made use of the equipment in the physiotherapy department to strengthen her weakened leg muscles.

It was four o'clock when Mrs Simmons interrupted their tea to tell Sandie she was wanted downstairs. Sandie rose to go with a smile at Donna, hoping she didn't look as nervous as she felt.

The two women sat facing each other on opposite side of the fireplace. Their faces showed nothing. If there had been any animosity between them there was no sign of it now, though they looked far from friendly. Eve was first to speak.

'We thought you would like to be first to know that Donna is to return to the States with her grandmother for a trial period,' she said coolly. 'It seems quite clear that she doesn't want to go to the school I've arranged for her. Mrs Fenning and I have talked it over and we agree that this is the best way.'

'And again, this is subject to Donna's approval,' Mrs Fenning put in. 'If you agree that she is fit enough to make the choice I should like to go up and ask her now.'

Sandie nodded. 'Of course, you will have to check with a doctor that she is fit to travel,' she advised. 'At the moment she is still convalescent.' She smiled. 'I'll be glad to make an appointment for you. She's having her tea at the moment, but I'm sure she'd love to see you if you want to go up.'

Eve stood and walked to the window. 'You go, Mona. I'm sure you're itching to give her the glad news,' she said without turning. 'I'll go up and say goodbye to her before I leave.'

When the door closed behind Mrs Fenning, Eve lit a cigarette and began to walk up and down. Sandie made a move towards the door but Eve said,

'Wait. They don't need either of us at the moment.' She shrugged impatiently. 'God knows I've done all I can for the child. Her father wanted her to be brought up and educated in this country and I've done my best to carry out his wishes, but I seem to have wasted my time. I hate to admit defeat but what's the use of fighting a losing battle? Obviously this is for the best.'

Sandie sat down. 'I'm sure you're right. Donna doesn't seem cut out for a stage career. She'll be happier in her native country.'

Eve stopped pacing and ground out her half-smoked cigarette in the ashtray on the coffee table, glancing speculatively at Sandie as she did so. 'Drew telephoned me last night,' she said suddenly. 'He said you'd been there.' Sandie looked up sharply and Eve smiled. 'Oh, it's all right, my dear. I'm a woman of the world. I know how it feels to be in love with a man you can never have. I admire you for doing all you can to get him. There's more fight in you than I thought. I saw that this morning. Believe me, you have all my sympathy.'

Sandie frowned. 'I'm sorry, I don't under-stand—'

'I thought at first it was just a crush,' Eve went on. 'But now I believe that your feelings are deep and genuine. Drew is a kind man. I'm sure he's fond of you and I know he'd never do or say anything to hurt you, but you must realise that there could never be any sort of future for you with him.'

Sandie could scarcely believe her ears. Could Drew really have telephoned Eve the moment she had left and told her everything that had passed between them? It was total betrayal. Eve crossed the room and sat beside her on the settee.

'Please, Sandie, don't look like that. I'm one of Drew's oldest friends, it's only natural that he should come to me for advice. I promised him I would let you down lightly, try to explain to you. He feels very guilty about possibly misleading you. You see, he's really very vulnerable. You're a very attractive girl and he was obviously flattered by your attention—not to say tempted. But Drew will never marry—not now. He's far too dedicated to his career. A girl like you should have a bright young husband and children. Drew is the first to recognise that. You shouldn't be wasting your time dreaming of someone as remote and unattainable as him.'

Sandie was stunned. She tried to tell herself that what Eve was saying was untrue—that Drew couldn't possibly have betrayed her so thoughtlessly; yet how else would Eve know she had been there, or what had passed between them? It was as she had feared. Drew must have had second thoughts after she had left, regretted the things he had said to her and panicked, running to Eve to get him out of what he now saw as a difficult and embarrassing situation. Sandie bit her lip as the humiliation of it overwhelmed her. How could she go back to Hartmoor General now? How could she ever live down the shame of the way she had flung herself at him? It would be intolerable.

Eve was looking at her hard. 'Sandie, my dear, I know what you must be feeling, believe me. It's going to be hard for you to see him again, isn't it? Not only hard, but painful. Will you let me help? I think I might have the perfect answer.'

Sandie couldn't trust herself to speak as she

looked at Eve. How could there be a perfect answer? She had looked forward to her job at Hartmoor General, yet right from the first she had been at a disadvantage. She had had no opportunity to make new friends—apart from Jenny and Tommy Bryant she had hardly met anyone. Then there had been the unfortunate 'Hartmoor Angel' publicity—that had done nothing to gain her popularity. Lastly, she had been assigned to the special outside job of nursing Donna. All of it had made her seem privileged, though none of it was her doing. The best thing, the *only* thing, was to hand in her notice and try to make a fresh start elsewhere. Eve laid a hand on her arm.

'I know how you feel. Whatever you might think, it's going to be hard for me to give up Donna. I'm letting her go with a good grace though, because I know that it's best for her. Can you perhaps try to feel the same way about Drew?' She reached out to press Sandie's hand. 'Now listen, Mona needs someone to help with Donna. She still runs her late husband's business, you see. If that person were to be you, a girl I know and trust, I'd feel happier about letting her go. And I know Mona would be delighted to have you.'

Sandie stared at her. 'Go to America, you mean? But I couldn't. There's Maddie to begin with—I couldn't leave her.'

'Maddie needs to lead her own life,' Eve said. 'Maybe I shouldn't repeat this, but she told me she felt responsible for you. I think the time has come for the two of you to break loose, Sandie. In the States you'd have the chance to make a completely fresh start. At least think it over, sleep on it.'

But Sandie didn't sleep at all that night. Eve had left after dinner to drive back to London. Donna and her grandmother were already making plans for their new life together and Mona had already approached Sandie about joining them—prompted, no doubt, by Eve. An appointment had been made for Donna at the hospital for tomorrow. Everything was moving so fast.

'Provided Donna gets a clean bill of health I'd like to go home as soon as possible,' Mona told her. 'I can't leave the business for too long, you see. Of course, I realise that you won't be able to get your visa and work permit in time to go with us and you may still need time to think things over, but if you could ring or cable just as soon as you decide, I'd be thrilled.'

Staring into the darkness, Sandie thought about it. Try as she would, she couldn't envisage a life away from England—from everything she knew and loved, and from Drew. Yet to stay here would be unthinkable after what had happened. There was her nursing, too. Fond as she was of Donna, she couldn't help but see the new arrangement as a waste of her skills. Mona had made so many tempting offers—her own flat, a car, holidays at the family cottage on Cape Cod . . .

Most girls would have seized the opportunity with both hands. But most girls weren't in love with Drew Maxwell, Sandie told herself despairingly. Deep in her heart the pain of his betrayal smarted like an open wound. How could he have telephoned Eve the moment she left the flat, begging her to get him off the hook? It was so cowardly and brutal. She buried her anguished face in the pillow.

If only she could hate him as he deserved to be hated. If only the agonising ache in her heart would go away!

She drove Donna and her grandmother into Hartmoor the following morning to keep the appointment with the surgeon who was standing in for Drew. Leaving them in the waiting-room, she went in search of Jenny. Finding that she was on nights she went across to the nurses' home, hoping she wasn't already in bed and asleep. She found her rinsing out some undies in the laundry-room.

'Sandie! How nice to see you. Are you coming back? Is the child wonder better?' Jenny's bright eyes danced, then she noticed Sandie's pale face and her smile faded.

'What on earth have they been doing to you?' She dried her hands. 'Come back to my room with me and I'll put the kettle on. You look as though you could do with a strong cup of coffee!'

In her room Jenny swept a pile of clothes off a chair and briskly tidied up. 'Sorry about the mess. I wasn't expecting company. Now, when can we expect you back?' She filled the kettle and plugged it in, turning to Sandie expectantly.

'That's why I've come to see you. I may not be coming back at all,' Sandie told her. Jenny sat down on the bed, eyebrows raised enquiringly.

'How's that? What's happened?'

'Donna's grandmother arrived unexpectedly from America,' Sandie explained. 'She's taking her back there to live, and she's asked me to go too.'

Jenny leaned back and let out her breath in a long, low whistle. 'Pheeew! Some people get all the luck!' She grinned wryly at Sandie. 'No doubt she's a fabulously wealthy woman and you'll have your own private swimming-pool and the use of the executive jet!'

'Not quite, though it does sound tempting,' Sandie said flatly.

Jenny frowned. 'Then how come you're not turning cartwheels? Why the long face? It can't be because you can't bear the thought of not seeing Sister Milton again!' She narrowed her eyes perceptively. 'Ah, of course, it's still Maxie, isn't it?'

Sandie shook her head. She hadn't come here to weep on Jenny's shoulder. 'It's nothing I won't get over. I dare say there'll be plenty to take my mind off it in America,' she said without conviction.

'You can say that again!' Jenny grinned. 'I'd quite envy you if my own life wasn't looking so bright.'

'Why, what's been happening while I've been away?' Sandie looked up with interest and was surprised to see that Jenny's cheeks had coloured prettily.

'You'll never believe this, but it's Tommy.'

Sandie stared at her. 'Tommy? Tommy Bryant, you mean? But I thought you two had some sort of feud going.'

'A love-hate relationship,' Jenny corrected. 'They say that the line between the two is very thin—well, we crossed it last week. I never thought I'd admit it to anyone, but I'm crazy about him. Isn't it funny? You can know someone for years and then suddenly one day you look at each other and *bingo!*'

Sandie laughed and hugged her. 'Well, at least that's one piece of good news. When you see

Tommy tell him I said he has more sense than I gave him credit for!'

'It's all thanks to you in a way,' Jenny told her.

'Me? Why me?'

'When he took you out I suddenly found that I minded,' Jenny confessed. 'Somehow I couldn't help showing it and Tommy was over the moon. He said he'd been trying to make me jealous for years and almost given up!'

Later there was more good news. Donna was discharged as fit to make the trip back to America, though Mona was given strict instructions to keep up the physiotherapy once they got home. As they drove back to Elm Court, Mona was bubbling over with plans and Donna looked happier than Sandie had ever seen her. Neither of them noticed her own drawn face or her silence as she drove.

It was four days later that Sandie drove Donna and Mona Fenning to the airport. Eve had said she would be there to see them off but at the last minute she had telephoned to say that she couldn't get away. Mona confessed to Sandie that she wasn't sorry.

'I've said all along the money was her prime consideration,' she confided. 'My son was besotted with her, of course, and I thank God he never saw through her as I did. She soon agreed to allow me to take Donna when I told her she needn't pay back the money left for the child's education. So much for her undying devotion!'

Sandie waved as their plane took off, then collected Maddie's car and drove into London to make the necessary arrangements for her coming trip to

America. It took longer than she had envisaged and it was quite late by the time she arrived back in Hartmoor, but although she was tired she called in at the hospital. Now that she had made up her mind to go, the sooner she gave in her notice, the better.

Mary Crawford, the SNO, was dismayed to hear that she intended to leave.

'Have you really given the matter enough thought?' she pressed. 'I can see that it's a tempting offer, but have you thought how out of touch with your nursing you'll get? And what about your stepmother? She's going to have quite a shock when she gets back from her holiday, isn't she?'

Sandie shook her head. 'Madeleine would never do anything to stand in my way.' She lowered her eyes. 'I'd like to ask you a favour. May I please be assigned to a medical ward while I'm working out my notice?'

Mary Crawford pursed her lips, leaning back in her chair to look at Sandie thoughtfully. 'Look, is there anything you want to talk about? Maybe I could help. You know that anything you told me would be treated with strict confidence.'

But Sandie shook her head. 'Everything's fine, thank you, really.'

'Is there someone you wish to avoid?'

Sandie swallowed hard. 'Well, yes.'

When she offered no more information Mary Crawford shook her head. 'Well, if there's anything I can do you know you only have to ask.' She smiled ruefully at Sandie. 'And I hardly need add that if you change your mind about leaving I shall be only too pleased.' She looked up. 'If you'd care to get back into harness tomorrow morning we're a staff nurse short on Men's Medical.'

It felt good to be back in uniform again next day and the busy routine helped to take Sandie's mind off her unhappiness. During her lunch-break she saw Jenny snatching a quick snack with Tommy Bryant in the canteen. Looking at their shining faces, she felt a pang of envy and turned away, but it was too late—they had already spotted her and beckoned her across to where they sat.

'So you're back! That's great,' Jenny said. 'Tommy and I were just planning a little party for Saturday evening, to celebrate our engagement. We'd love you to come, wouldn't we, Tommy?'

Tommy grinned. 'Of course. It's only an informal do in The Feathers. There'll be drinks and a buffet. Come about nine.'

Sandie hesitated. 'Well, it's kind of you to ask me, of course, but I don't think I'm very good company at the moment.'

'Oh do come,' Jenny looked at her watch. 'Damn, I haven't got time to twist your arm now. Sister Johns on Gynae goes a delicate shade of puce if you're five seconds late.' She stood up and bent to kiss Tommy. 'See you later, darling. Don't let Sandie go till she's promised to come to the party, will you?'

When she had gone, Sandie slid into the seat opposite Tommy. She smiled at him. 'I'm really glad about you two. You're absolutely right for each other.'

'We're both barmy, you mean?' He grinned ruefully at her. 'I've been in love with Jenny ever since we were mixed infants together. It was a case of her not being able to see the wood for the trees.' He reached across to touch her arm. 'You're looking a bit peaky, love. Nothing wrong, is there?'

She avoided his searching eyes. 'Of course not. I'm fine.'

'About that evening at The Kingfisher,' he said. 'I got a rocket from Drew. I hope he wasn't too tough on you. I told him the whole thing was my fault.'

There was a huge lump in Sandie's throat and her chest ached with the effort of keeping the tears back. If only he wouldn't keep on about Drew. It was like a knife twisting in her heart.

'He was a bit cross, but it didn't matter,' she said with a shrug. 'Jenny has probably told you that I'm off to America soon, anyway.'

He regarded her for a long moment, his eyes thoughtful. Being engaged seemed to have made him a much more perceptive person. 'I wish I knew why you were going, Sandie—and whether it might be because I did anything to spoil things for you. Going out with you was what tipped the scales for Jenny and me. I feel I owe you, and I know that you and Drew—'

'Oh, Tommy, *please*!' She stopped him in midsentence, biting her lip hard. 'Look, you had nothing to do with it, really. Now, what would you and Jenny like as a wedding present? As I shan't be here I'd better get on and buy it.'

'You *will* be coming to the party then? You must if you won't be at the wedding.'

She stood up. 'All right. I'll try to look in for a while. If you have a present list will you let me see it? Bye for now.' And she escaped as quickly as she could.

The following day in her lunch-break, Sandie slipped out to the shops. She had seen just the thing for Jenny and Tommy in a shop close to the hospital—a bone china tea-set with a delicate pattern of wild roses. She was walking back across the car park, carrying the large, gift-wrapped box, when a familiar car caught her eye. It was Drew's dark blue saloon, parked in the space reserved for him, and her heart missed a beat as she saw him get out and lock the door. Catching her breath she drew back out of sight, her heart aching as she watched him stride across the forecourt and disappear into the building. So he was back. Would he try to see her, to make some sort of explanation? How embarrassing if he did. She would do all she could to avoid him. He wasn't officially due back until Monday, but she would be on her guard.

There were three telephone calls for her at the nurses' home but she refused to take any of them, telling the girl who answered to say she was out. Once she saw Drew in the corridor talking to another doctor and only just slipped out of sight in time. She wondered how she would keep it up for the next three weeks. It was inevitable that they would meet some time—but not yet if she could avoid it, not until she felt strong enough to handle it.

On Saturday evening there was a tap on her door and Jenny whisked into the room as Sandie was washing her hair.

'Well, what do you think?' Her cheeks were pink and her eyes shining as she twirled for Sandie's approval. She wore a new dress of sky blue that exactly matched her eyes, and her blonde hair curled softly round her face.

Sandie wrapped a towel round her head and straightened up to look at her friend. 'You look lovely. Being engaged certainly suits you.' She reached into the wardrobe. 'Here, I'd like you to have this now.'

Jenny took the large box from her doubtfully. 'Oh, but you *are* coming to the party, aren't you? Tommy said—'

Sandie smiled. 'Yes, of course I am. I just wanted you to have your present now. Open it and see if you like it. If you don't you can change it.'

'I suppose I should really wait for Tommy,' Jenny began to tear off the wrapping excitedly, 'but I can't wait to see! Oh!' She held up one of the pretty cups. 'Oh, Sandie, it's *gorgeous*. It must have cost the earth. You really shouldn't!'

Sandie smiled. 'I might not be here when you get married, so this is to double as an engagement and wedding present.'

Jenny sat sown on the bed with a sigh. 'Oh dear, I do wish you weren't going. I can't really believe you want to. There are as good fish in the sea, you know.'

Sandie turned away, towelling her hair vigorously to hide her face. Jenny stood up, picking up the box.

'Oh well, maybe something will happen to make you change your mind. Thanks again for the lovely present, Sandie. See you later.'

Sandie finished drying her hair and pinned it up into a tight chignon, then she took out her velvet skirt and a crisp white silk blouse. She had decided to look in at the party early and get it over with. As more people started to arrive no one would notice when she slipped quietly away. As she made up her face she noticed for the first time how pale her cheeks were and the sharpening of the bones beneath the skin. When would Drew's betrayal stop hurting? she wondered. So far there was no lessening of the pain, especially now that she knew he was back in Hartmoor. As the days went by the tension was growing unbearable.

The lounge bar at The Feathers looked festive and when Sandie arrived there were already a dozen people there. As soon as she saw her, Jenny rushed over, taking both her hands and pulling her across to where Tommy stood.

'Come and be thanked for your super present,' she said, her eyes dancing. 'Tommy was knocked out by it, weren't you, darling?'

'It's lovely.' Tommy seized her and glanced at Jenny. 'May I kiss her, just this once?' he asked, his eyes twinkling. 'After all, I'll soon be an old married man!' He kissed Sandie swiftly, then asked, 'What can I get you to drink? Let me make you one of my special cocktails. That should bring the colour back to your cheeks!'

Sandie began to relax. She chatted to people she had only previously known by sight and soon found she was more popular than she had imagined. Suddenly her Hartmoor Angel title was a joke and she began to think she had been foolish to see it any other way. Everyone wanted to know about Donna and what it was like to nurse the daughter of a celebrity. The time flew. One hour passed, then another, and Sandie quite forgot her resolution to leave early. She was talking to Graham Blake, the stocky, grey-haired radiologist, when a movement over by the door caught her eye and her heart almost stopped. A late guest had just arrived. There was no mistaking the tall figure and the dark head with its distinctive silver streak. Graham was looking at her panic-stricken face with concern.

'What is it? Anything wrong?'

'Oh, I feel a little faint. I think I'll go outside for some fresh air.' She began to make her way towards the door, but she was only half-way there when Jenny caught her arm.

'Sandie! Where are you off to?' The other girl looked at her closely. 'It isn't because of someone who's just arrived, is it? Surely you don't have to run and hide from him?'

'Of course not, don't be silly,' Sandie said breathlessly, trying to shake off Jenny's hand. 'I feel a bit faint, that's all. It's later than I thought and I—Oh!' Drew had seen her and was making his way towards her, a purposeful look in his eye. Jenny took in the situation at a glance.

'I'm afraid it's too late to escape. Whatever it is, you're going to have to face it out. Well, I'll leave you to it.' And she melted into the crowd.

Sandie felt rooted to the spot. She glanced again towards the door, wondering whether to make a last desperate effort to make it, but a moment later she felt Drew's hand close firmly round her arm. She turned to look up into his eyes and saw that he was angry.

'I think it might be easier to talk outside,' he said, steering her towards the door.

After the heat in the bar the night air was chilly, but the tremor that went through her had nothing to do with the evening breeze. Drew's hand still held her fast. He drew her into a shadowy corner and looked down at her.

'Why have you been avoiding me? I think you owe me an explanation, don't you? I left you in charge of one of my patients and now I find she's left the country and you're back here, without a single word to me!'

She was shaking. 'There was nothing I could do about it. Her grandmother wanted to take her, Eve agreed—it was out of my hands. I did make sure she was checked to see that she was fit to travel.'

His fingers were like steel and beginning to hurt as they pressed into the flesh of her arm. 'And you're joining them in America, I hear, again from a third party!'

She looked up at him. It was dark but she could just make out the strong lines of his face and the smouldering anger in his eyes. 'I—I thought it would be best if I got out of your way,' she said shakily. 'Mrs Fenning offered me the job, so I took it.'

He let go her arm to grasp both her shoulders. 'I can't begin to understand this. When I ring you I'm told you're out. When you see me coming you slip out of sight. Didn't it occur to you to talk to me before you took so drastic a step?'

'No! Not after the message you sent me. Why should I ask you?'

The door of the bar opened and a group of noisy revellers spilled out, laughing and shouting to each other as they made their way to the car park. Drew took her arm decisively:

'We'll go to the flat,' he told her. 'It's only five minutes away. We can't talk here.' She made a feeble protest but he wasn't listening. Striding across to where his car was parked, he took her with him.

They drove in silence, but as Sandie glanced at his profile she saw that he was furious—almost as furious as the night he took her home from The Kingfisher. Her own anger rose too. What right had he to expect her to consult him before she took a new job?

As he closed the door of the flat he looked at her. 'You're cold—your teeth are chattering. I'll switch the fire on. Do you want coffee?'

'I want to go home,' she said, trying to control her trembling. 'So if you can just say whatever it is you've brought me here to say, maybe I—' She gasped as he grasped her shoulders, glowering down at her.

'Sandie! Just what *is* the matter with you? The last time you were here—'

'Last time I was here I very nearly made a complete fool of myself and I'd rather not be reminded of it, thank you!' She was almost in tears. 'It must have embarrassed you dreadfully for you to feel obliged to send another woman to warn me off, but I don't think *you* have any right to complain about hearing things through a third party!'

He shook his head, eyes blazing. 'You're talking in riddles! I don't even begin to understand any of this. Will you kindly tell me what you're talking about, or do I have to *shake* it out of you?'

'All right! You rang Eve that night!' she almost shouted at him. 'The moment I left here you rang her.'

He frowned. 'That's right, I rang her.'

She stared at him, momentarily taken aback. 'You rang her to ask her to let me down lightly. That was the way she put it.'

His brow darkened. 'I haven't the slightest idea what you mean. I rang Eve to tell her that her mother-in-law had arrived. I explained that you'd been here and that you'd had a call.'

Sandie looked at him guardedly. 'But that wasn't all you told her, was it?'

For a long moment he stood looking down at her, his grip on her shoulders slackening. 'From certain things you told me that evening I realised that Eve had lied to me. I told her I'd made a decision, that now Donna had made a complete recovery I wanted our friendship to end.'

'Oh.' Sandie stared up at him, stunned. Suddenly it was all so clear. Eve must have put two and two together. Afraid that she was losing Drew, she had made a last, desperate attempt at getting him back, planning to remove Sandie as far as possible from him. And she had almost succeeded! Drew was looking at her.

'Didn't you see through what she was trying to do? Didn't you trust me?'

She shook her head. 'All I could think of was the way I'd flung myself at you. I felt so cheap. I didn't see how I could ever face you again.'

He pulled her into his arms. 'So that was why you kept scuttling round corners and pretending to be out when I rang. Can't you see, darling, that if what

Eve told you was true, it would be I who should feel cheap?' He raised her face to look into her eyes. 'There was so much I planned to say to you that evening, if only that damned phone hadn't rung!'

'Do you think you could say it to me now, please?' she whispered.

He looked at her for a long moment. 'I meant to tell you that I couldn't pretend any more, Sandie,' he said softly. 'That I couldn't get you out of my mind or out of my life. That I didn't even want to try any more.'

She held her breath. 'What you're trying to say is—is that you—'

'Is that I love you, yes.' He pulled her close with a sigh. 'It makes no more sense than it did before, but I know now that I have to face the fact that it's real and it's not going to go away.' He looked down at her, his eyes tender. 'I think we've both got to admit that there's only one cure for it, Sandie.' His arms closed round her, crushing her close, and his lips came down on hers. As they drew apart his eyes searched hers.

'Once I stopped you saying you loved me. It would serve me right if you'd stopped after all that's happened.'

She touched his face tenderly, tracing the fine lines at the corners of his eyes and the hardness of his cheekbones. 'No, I haven't stopped,' she whispered breathlessly. 'I never will. All I've ever wanted was to prove that to you, but something always seemed to get in the way.' His lips found hers again and she melted in the warmth and mounting passion of his kiss, all the pain of the past days dissolving away. He raised his head to look anxiously at her.

'God, I've just thought! How far have you got with your arrangements to leave for the States?'

She smiled and shook her head. 'I never even told Mrs Fenning for sure that I would accept her offer. So far all I've done is to make enquiries about a visa and give in my notice.'

'Phew! What a relief!' He kissed her. 'There's something else you haven't done—you haven't said you'll marry me yet. I'd like to hear you say it, please.'

She slipped her arms round his waist and pressed her face against his chest. 'Of course I will.'

He began to pull the pins out of her hair. 'And do I get another chance?'

She looked up and saw the ghost of a twinkle in his eyes.

'All that "throwing yourself at me" as you put it; it wasn't my fault if it never came off. Would you mind very much trying it again—with my help, of course?' He raked his fingers through the tawny mass of her hair as it tumbled over her shoulders. 'I'm not officially on duty till Monday,' he whispered, kissing the tip of her nose. 'If the telephone rings this time it can go on ringing!' He looked at his watch. 'We've got thirty-six hours to make up for lost time. It's not long, but it's a start.'

She wound her arms happily round his neck. 'Yes, darling—it's a start,' she agreed. 'A wonderful start!'

Mills & Boon

4 Doctor Nurse Romances
FREE

Coping with the daily tragedies and ordeals of a busy hospital, and sharing the satisfaction of a difficult job well done, people find themselves unexpectedly drawn together. Mills & Boon Doctor Nurse Romances capture perfectly the excitement, the intrigue and the emotions of modern medicine, that so often lead to overwhelming and blissful love. By becoming a regular reader of Mills & Boon Doctor Nurse Romances you can enjoy EIGHT superb new titles every two months plus a whole range of special benefits: your very own personal membership card, a free newsletter packed with recipes, competitions, bargain book offers, plus big cash savings.

**AND an Introductory FREE GIFT for YOU.
Turn over the page for details.**

**Fill in and send this coupon back today
and we'll send you
4 Introductory
Doctor Nurse Romances yours to keep**

FREE

At the same time we will reserve a
subscription to Mills & Boon
Doctor Nurse Romances for you. Every
two months you will receive the latest
8 new titles, delivered direct to your door.
You don't pay extra for delivery. Postage and
packing is always completely Free.
There is no obligation or commitment—
you receive books only for
as long as you want to.

**It's easy! Fill in the coupon below and return it to
MILLS & BOON READER SERVICE, FREEPOST, P.O. BOX 236,
CROYDON, SURREY CR9 9EL.**

**Please note: READERS IN SOUTH AFRICA write to
Mills & Boon Ltd., Postbag X3010,
Randburg 2125, S. Africa.**

FREE BOOKS CERTIFICATE

**To: Mills & Boon Reader Service, FREEPOST, P.O. Box 236,
Croydon, Surrey CR9 9EL.**

Please send me, free and without obligation, four Dr Nurse Romances, and reserve a
Reader Service Subscription for me. If I decide to subscribe I shall receive, following my free
parcel of books, eight new Dr Nurse Romances every two months for £8.00, post and
packing free. If I decide not to subscribe, I shall write to you within 10 days. The free books
are mine to keep in any case. I understand that I may cancel my subscription at any time
simply by writing to you. I am over 18 years of age.
Please write in BLOCK CAPITALS.

Name _____

Address _____

_____

_____ Postcode _____

SEND NO MONEY — TAKE NO RISKS

*Remember, postcodes speed delivery. Offer applies in UK only and is not valid to
present subscribers. Mills & Boon reserve the right to exercise discretion
in granting membership. If price changes are necessary you will be notified. Offer expires 31st December 1984.*

8DN